"This is a charmingly told story with some extremely likeable characters. Regency fans should adore this one." —Rakehell.com

"A charming tale!" —*Rendezvous*

"Endearing." —*Romantic Times*

Kiss of the Highwayman

"A surprisingly tender love story."—*Romantic Times*

Miranda's Mistake

"Another fabulous story from Miss Mindel, the queen of romance. Her tale of love has a wonderful plot, desire, and a longing ache for true love to conquer." —Under the Covers

The Captain's Secret

"Secrets, traitors to the crown, action, and danger add up to one of the most delightful books I have enjoyed this year! Very highly and thoroughly recommended!" —Huntress Reviews

Labor of Love

"A delicious blend of gentle humor and poignant heartache." —*Romantic Times*

Blessing in Disguise

"A delightful romance . . . a true reading pleasure." —Jo Beverley

"Warm, witty, and deliciously romantic—a splendid debut!" —Gail Eastwood

REGENCY ROMANCE
COMING IN DECEMBER 2005

Marry in Haste and Francesca's Rake
by Lynn Kerstan
Together for the first time, two Regency classics star heroines gambling on love, not knowing if they will lose their hearts—or win true love.

0-451-21717-9

Miss Clarkson's Classmate
by Sharon Sobel
Emily Clarkson arrives at her new teaching position expecting her employer to be a gentleman, and she's shocked to find a brute. He's expecting a somber old maid. And neither is expecting the passion that soon overtakes them both.

0-451-21718-7

Lady Emma's Dilemma
by Rhonda Woodward
Once lovers, Lady Emmaline and Baron Devreux have different points of view concerning their long-ago tryst. But in an unexpected encounter, the two simply have too many questions and the answers only come by moonlight—and with a little mischief.

0-451-21701-2

Available wherever books are sold or at penguin.com

Lord Grafton's Promise

Jenna Mindel

A SIGNET BOOK

SIGNET
Published by New American Library, a division of
Penguin Group (USA) Inc., 375 Hudson Street,
New York, New York 10014, USA
Penguin Group (Canada), 90 Eglinton Avenue East, Suite 700, Toronto,
Ontario M4P 2Y3, Canada (a division of Pearson Penguin Canada Inc.)
Penguin Books Ltd., 80 Strand, London WC2R 0RL, England
Penguin Ireland, 25 St. Stephen's Green, Dublin 2,
Ireland (a division of Penguin Books Ltd.)
Penguin Group (Australia), 250 Camberwell Road, Camberwell, Victoria 3124,
Australia (a division of Pearson Australia Group Pty. Ltd.)
Penguin Books India Pvt. Ltd., 11 Community Centre, Panchsheel Park,
New Delhi - 110 017, India
Penguin Group (NZ), cnr Airborne and Rosedale Roads, Albany,
Auckland 1310, New Zealand (a division of Pearson New Zealand Ltd.)
Penguin Books (South Africa) (Pty.) Ltd., 24 Sturdee Avenue,
Rosebank, Johannesburg 2196, South Africa

Penguin Books Ltd., Registered Offices:
80 Strand, London WC2R 0RL, England

First published by Signet, an imprint of New American Library,
a division of Penguin Group (USA) Inc.

First Printing, November 2005
10 9 8 7 6 5 4 3 2 1

To my editor, Rose Hilliard, who is so sharp and an absolute pleasure to work with.

To my agent, Pamela Harty, who is a peach and I am very glad she chose to represent me.

Thank you both, not only for believing in me, but cheering me on and guiding my steps.

Chapter One

" S hall we depart, my dear?" Sir Alaric Darrow extended his hand.

Lucinda Bronwell accepted his warm palm. He was a tall man, his straight stature barely touched by age. He had a headful of white hair cut short in the latest style. A fine-looking man of advanced years— her newly wed husband.

They rushed toward his closed carriage amid the cheers of family and friends. Fragrant rose petals thrown by the wedding guests fluttered about, scenting the cold, damp November air with heavy sweetness.

No expense had been spared for their wedding, even though it had been held at his nephew's manor in Coventry. The bridal trip would be simple—no more than an overnight stay at a luxurious inn on the way to Sir Alaric's country estate in Warwickshire.

Lucinda did not mind. She did not need an elaborate honeymoon. Her family had been generously provided for and she had accomplished what she had set out to do. She had married a terribly wealthy man even if he was old enough to be her grandfather.

Sir Alaric helped her step into the carriage. Once seated, he arranged a heavy deerskin rug over her lap. "The hot bricks should last until we reach the inn." He lifted two silver flasks out of a picnic basket on the seat next to him. "And what have we here? Something to warm our insides." He gave her a wink, but his smile wavered.

Lucinda felt the same nervousness as he. This evening required that they consummate their vows. Her mother, bless her heart, had given her timid instructions about how to go on, but even so, Lucinda barely governed her anxiety. She was adept at playing a role—she had done as much in London—but the marriage bed was no easy stage.

With a weak smile, she took the proffered flask from her husband, feeling she would have need of its contents. She leaned out the open window to wave one last time to her mother and her siblings.

Tears streamed down her mother's cheeks. In her mother's eyes, Lucinda recognized the shame she had learned to bury in order to do what must be done to save her family's home and her father's legacy. But seeing that shame so clearly reflected in her mother's face, Lucinda felt a twinge of doubt. Had there been any other way than this? She shook it off. What was done was done. Everyone knew she had married for money. The one to feel sorry for was the husband who sat across from her. He had dropped a tidy sum on a young wife who did not love him.

Lucinda gave her mother an encouraging nod. It would be all right. Sir Alaric was a patient man. He had proved as much by waiting nearly six months after he had offered for her to finally wed.

In those six months, the Bronwell finances had been put back to rights. Their ancestral home was safe from the auction block, her little brother attended Eton, and her two sisters were given dowries so that when their time came to experience a Season, they could each pursue a love match.

Lucinda glanced at Sir Alaric. Might she grow to love him in time? He possessed a dear heart despite his colorful past fraught with business schemes, rumored duels, and mistresses. Sir Alaric had been exceptionally kind to her and her family and that must count for something in the ways of the heart. He did not make her feel like what she was—a shameless fortune hunter. For that, she would forever be grateful.

He took a deep sip of the contents of his flask.

"What is it?" she asked.

"Brandy."

She wrinkled her nose. She did not care for strong spirits. "And in the basket?" It was not a long drive south to the inn and an even shorter distance beyond to Sir Alaric's estate of Ivy Park. They would hardly have need of food on their journey.

"Meat pies, cheese, and apples," he said. "Would you like some?"

"Thank you, no." Lucinda held her stomach. She had eaten well at their bridal breakfast. She couldn't swallow another morsel.

Sir Alaric took another swig from his flask and

mopped his brow with his handkerchief. His cheeks were flushed.

"I hope you haven't caught Bethany's sniffle." Lucinda's sister had been bedridden only a week before the wedding.

"Not that, surely." He quickly looked away.

She shifted in her seat. Trepidation about the night ahead settled in the carriage with a bad case of the fidgets. Sir Alaric continued to down the contents of the flask and Lucinda picked at the embroidered edge of the deerskin covering her. Finally, she took the cap off her own flask and took a sip. She needed courage.

The brandy burned its way down her throat, warding off the chill and settling her anxious fears. She would be just fine. Again, she looked at Sir Alaric.

"Do not worry, Lucy," he said quietly.

She knew her cheeks had turned red. She could feel the heat in her face. She hoped Sir Alaric would attribute the deepened color to the brandy or the cold and not the evening that hung before them. She nodded, then looked out of her window. She watched the passing landscape for quite some time before she noticed her husband's condition had worsened.

"Alaric, you do not look well." They were close to the inn, which gave Lucinda some assurance that at least they would soon be off the road and she could care for him.

"I do not know what's the trouble. I was fine this morning." He puffed and gasped and his breath was pungent. "I feel a little faint." His cheeks, flushed a deep red only moments before, looked pale as he mopped his sweat-soaked brow and licked his lips.

Lucinda felt nauseated. She could not be sure if it was due to the motion of the carriage or her husband's putrid breath. Either way, they needed to stop for fresh air.

She stood up and tapped upon the trapdoor. When it opened slightly, she yelled through the crack to the coachman, "You must stop the carriage. Sir Alaric is ill."

The trapdoor shut with a snap. Before she could sit down, the carriage swayed as they rounded a corner. Then it jerked and she was thrown against the far wall. They tumbled over and over, the contents of the carriage tossed about in wild abandon.

Lucinda bumped her head against the seat and her legs tangled with Sir Alaric's before the carriage finally ceased turning. She landed hard upon her back and her breath was forced out of her lungs with a sharp gasp.

She lay still, blinking her eyes in an attempt to focus on the carriage seats, which now hung above her head. She heard Sir Alaric cough and sputter in a struggle to breathe. He gulped at the air and wheezed.

"Alaric?" she whispered.

"You hurt?" he choked out.

"I do not think so." She pulled herself to a sitting position, her body stiff and aching from being thrown about. She turned around to check on him and the blood rushed from her head, making her dizzy. Panic rose in her throat but she forced it down. She must remain calm.

He lay twisted in a grotesque manner, with his legs turned out awkwardly and his arms draped across his chest. His face had turned an ashen gray color. His shallow gasps were wrought from him with immense effort. He could not move.

She crawled toward him. "What can I do?"

He stared at her, helpless. "Go, now."

Help! Of course, they needed help. She kicked open the door and crawled out onto the damp ground. Moisture from the long grass soaked through her skirt, chilling her instantly. She stood and circled the overturned carriage. "Coachman," she cried. "Coachman!" But there was no one.

He must have gone to fetch help. She dashed back into the carriage. Sir Alaric looked even worse and she had only been gone a few moments. She did not know what to do. "He's gone for help. Help will be here soon."

She tucked the deerskin around him, hoping it would ease the tremors that violently shook him.

"Run," he wheezed.

Confused, she stared at him. "I will not leave you."

And then she heard the sound of horse hooves in the distance. Help had arrived!

Douglas Alexander James Arden, Earl of Grafton, spotted an overturned carriage that lay with its wheels in the air a good stretch of road ahead. He urged his mount into a gallop and rushed to the scene.

The horses had broken away from the harness but remained tethered to their yoke. They stood a few yards away from the wreckage, munching grass as if nothing were out of the ordinary. Neither horse looked injured.

As he drew closer, he spotted a woman crawling

out. He recognized her instantly as the vulgar little fortune hunter who had thrown herself at every eligible man with deep pockets this past spring in London.

Miss Lucinda Bronwell ran toward him, frantically waving her arms, her guinea gold hair disheveled. "Please, please hurry."

His stallion, Horatio, was spooked to be so accosted. Grafton used a firm hand to keep his mount from rearing and causing Miss Bronwell harm. "Get back, madam!"

She did not heed him, but drew closer, clawing at his booted foot with a wild look in her huge blue eyes. "My husband"—she nearly choked on the word—"is badly hurt."

He quickly gained control over Horatio and dismounted. He vaguely remembered reading about her upcoming nuptials to his neighbor Sir Alaric Darrow, in the *Morning Post*. He should have recalled when the two had wed—he had sent his regrets soon after receiving an invitation. He followed her as she scurried back to the overturned carriage.

"Alaric is inside and he's— You must help him!" Her voice broke into a sob and she buried her face in her hands.

He laid a hand upon her shoulder and squeezed, hoping to offer some comfort; then he darted into the carriage. Dull light streamed in from the windows. He immediately smelled a foul scent like garlic but more shocking than the odor was the sight of the man whose lands bordered his own.

Sir Alaric Darrow, an age-old friend of his father's, lay twisted and gasping. His eyes bulged with a glassy appearance that did not bode well for any hope of recovery. Unfortunately, Grafton had witnessed death before and Sir Alaric bore the telltale signs of a man about to die.

He quickly stripped off his greatcoat and bundled it under the older man's head.

"Grafton," Sir Alaric hissed.

" 'Tis I."

"Lucy . . . away." His voice was ragged and his breath rancid.

Even so, Grafton bent lower to hear him better. Sir Alaric did not move his twisted legs and his hands were curled into claws that lay unmoving upon his chest. It took a tremendous effort for him to speak.

"Danger."

Grafton patted the older man's shoulder. "She is fine. In fact, your wife is waiting outside. We shall have you out of here in no time."

Sir Alaric widened his eyes in a silent plea.

Grafton thought the man had run mad, yet Sir Alaric's fear had nothing to do with death's door. Something was terribly wrong. "What is it?"

"Flask." Sir Alaric's eyes rolled toward the door.

Grafton followed his gaze until he saw the silver canister. He grabbed the flask and lifted it for Sir Alaric to see. Grafton was horrified when a shuddering spasm took hold of Sir Alaric. He waited for the tremors to stop. White foam appeared at the corners of Sir Alaric's mouth and he choked and gurgled. His condition did not have the appearance of simply a broken neck.

Grafton looked at the flask he held in his hand. He unscrewed the lid and sniffed. It smelled only of strong spirits.

"Poison," Sir Alaric said almost clearly.

Grafton felt as if he'd been kicked in the gut. "Where did you get this?"

"Protect Lucy."

Good God! Grafton stared at him. What was he saying?

"Promise!"

"Yes, yes, I promise—upon my honor." Grafton quickly placed the flask in the pocket of his jacket. He would have the contents checked.

Sir Alaric visibly relaxed. It was close to the end. "Your father—proud."

Grafton's spine stiffened. "Sir Alaric," he whispered, "who did this?"

Too late.

Helpless, Grafton watched as Sir Alaric's eyes rolled back into his head and he breathed his last with a shuddering shake. Grafton bowed his head and silently prayed a blessing over the body before pulling the deerskin rug up to cover Sir Alaric's face.

"I give you my word, I will find out who did this to you." Anger sliced through him with white-hot intensity. Sir Alaric, rogue though he may have been, did not deserve such an end.

"Is he . . . ?"

Grafton turned to see Sir Alaric's wife, Lucinda, peeking through the opened door. Tears streamed down her dusty face. Her bonnet had fallen past her shoulders, held in place by a bow of white ribbon. Sections of her tangled hair fell about her face, and by all that was holy, her bright blue eyes looked hopeful.

"What happened here?" he whispered.

Her eyes opened wider. "Wh-what do you mean? The carriage has turned over."

"Where's your coachman?" he asked.

"He must have gone for help. How is Alaric?"

"Your husband is dead, madam. I am sorry."

Pain flickered across her face before she covered her mouth with her hand and backed away.

He crawled out of the carriage in time to see Lucinda stumble away from him, only to fall to her knees and wretch.

Grafton fingered the flask in his pocket. He waited until her illness finally subsided. He stepped beside her and offered his handkerchief.

"Thank you," she mumbled. She would not look at him.

Grafton showed her the flask. "Did you drink from this?"

She looked at him then. "Yes."

"How much did you drink?"

"A sip is all, to ward off the chill." Fear shone from her eyes. "Why?"

"Sir Alaric was poisoned."

Her eyes closed and she clutched her stomach and cast up her accounts once again. Her shoulders shook and Grafton prayed he would not have to witness another scene like what he had seen in the carriage. Surely she had not ingested as much of the poison as her husband.

She wiped her mouth with his handkerchief and her hands trembled. Her face was pale and distressed, and her huge eyes brimmed with tears.

He reached out his hand. "Come, you cannot stay here."

"Where are we going?" She took a step closer but stumbled.

Awkwardly, he wrapped an arm about her shoulders and led her to his horse. "My home is not far from here."

"But what about Alaric?"

"I will return with my men."

"I cannot leave him." She pulled away and headed back for the carriage.

He moved quickly and stood in front of the open door, barring her way. "You cannot stay here alone."

"But the coachman will return."

"Is he Sir Alaric's servant?"

"I do not know."

"Where did you get the flask?"

She stepped away from him and rubbed her forehead as if she had difficulty remembering. "From the picnic basket."

His patience grew thin. "Madam, who prepared the basket?"

"I do not know. It was in the carriage after our wedding breakfast. I cannot be sure who gave it to us. I did not see a note."

"*Today* is your wedding day?" Grafton could not believe his ears. How cursed foul to kill a man on his bridal trip.

She looked up at him, tears spilling over the red rims of her eyes. "Yes."

She started to cry with quick whimpering sobs and Grafton knew he had to get her out of the cold and into his mother's care.

Grafton continued to stare, unsure whether to comfort her or throw her across his saddle. She had married Sir Alaric for his money—it was no secret. In fact, the whole village was abuzz with that bit of gossip. Now the news of Sir Alaric's death, an apparent murder, would be the talk of the town. Grafton could not help but wonder if Lucinda Bronwell was bold enough to kill her husband on their wedding day.

Chapter Two

Warwickshire

*L*ucinda sat stiffly in the saddle. She tried not to lean too hard into the gentleman behind her, but she was cold and he was warm. He looked familiar but she could not recall his name. She racked her memory until she remembered that she had met him at a dinner party in London this past Season. He was a high-and-mighty nobleman who believed himself better than most. Arrogance had reeked from him.

As suspicion did now.

After some time sharing the saddle in silence, she worked up the courage to ask, "Might you tell me who you are and where we are headed?"

"Forgive me. I assumed that you knew. I am Lord Grafton and we are headed to Arden Hall, my home. My land lies adjacent to Sir Alaric's." The timbre of his voice was deep. She felt it rumble from inside his chest as she leaned against him purely for the sake of warmth. She was chilled to bone and trembling besides.

Of course! How could she have forgotten his name?
He was a paragon of virtue, but also a man of con-
descension. She had grown used to being looked
down upon. Wearing indecent décolletage and sheer
gowns in order to catch the attentions of a wealthy
man was something she felt she had to do, but she
did not have to like lowering herself to such machinations.

And now her rich husband was dead and Lord
Grafton wondered if she was to blame. How many
others would believe her capable of murder?

Grafton felt her tremble within the circle of his
arms and he was sorely tempted to stop at the inn
and let her get warm while he hired a hackney. But
that would take too much time. He urged his mount
into a canter. The faster they reached Arden Hall,
the better.

She slipped in the saddle when the horse changed
its gait. He pulled her close to steady her, his arm
wrapped firmly around her waist. Her hair flew into
his face and her flowery scent wafted into his
nostrils.

"Don't want you to fall," he said close to her ear.

She remained silent, but nodded, both her hands
clutching his arm.

It was difficult not to notice how good she felt
pressed against him. He had never been one to dally
with light skirts, but he was not immune to an attrac-
tive woman. Lucinda Bronwell was beautiful, even
more so than he remembered, but then he had done
everything in his power to ignore her since the min-
ute they had met.

He clearly recalled sitting in his assigned seat next

to her at a dinner party. He had been deeply disappointed with his placement because he wished to pay court to Miss Whitlow, who had been seated farther down the same table.

Miss Bronwell had annoyed him to no end with her endless chatter and attempts to capture his attention with the swell of her bosom.

"Lord Grafton, my name is Lucinda Bronwell. 'Tis nice to make your acquaintance." She bent low over the table in order that he might take pleasure in her form.

He tried to focus on her face, but her gown dipped so low at the bodice that his gaze continually strayed to the swell of creamy flesh displayed for one and all.

He had been dashed uncomfortable the whole evening and it had been hard not to look. Most of the fellows ogled her outright, but he could hardly do something that coarse. So he had done his best to gaze elsewhere, but failed. He remembered sneaking any number of peeks at her, all the while inwardly cursing her for her lack of modesty.

She was the epitome of vulgar in her obvious hunt for a wealthy husband. The type of man did not matter so long as his pockets were lined with gold. Marrying Sir Alaric proved how indiscriminate her choice had been.

And now Grafton was honor bound to take her into his home and protect her! His reputation would no doubt suffer, but he had given his word as a gentleman.

When they arrived at Arden Hall, they rode down a long drive that led to a magnificent Elizabethan home. It was built with gray stone and mullioned glass windows that reflected rainbows in the dwindling rays of sunshine peeking through the dark clouds above. The structure stood on a small hill that sloped gently to a tiny lake beyond the front of the house. Extensive gardens bordered the home on each side.

Lights shone from some of the windows and Lucinda hoped someone other than his lordship lived here. She did not think Lord Grafton had married or surely she would have heard. In spite of his high-handed demeanor, he was one of the most desired bachelors on the marriage mart in London. He would hardly allow her to enter a bachelor's establishment alone—he was far too proper for that. Perhaps he planned to ship her off to Ivy Park once she was warm and dry.

The horse's hooves crunched upon dried-up brown leaves swirled across the graveled drive as they approached the stables. The crisp smell of wood smoke filled the air.

Two groomsmen darted out to give them aid, and they both stopped when they saw her, their eyes wide. She must look a perfect fright.

Lord Grafton gave quick orders. "Make ready a wagon. We must travel just past the Rose and Slipper Inn as soon as I return." Then he slid off his horse and reached out to her. His large hands easily spanned her waist as he lifted her down.

When her feet hit the ground, her knees gave out and she nearly ended up on the ground. Ever the gentleman, Lord Grafton swept her up into his arms. She did not know what to say, since he did not appear pleased by having to hold her, so she remained quiet.

It was awkward enough to ride several miles plastered against the solid wall of him with his arm draped around her waist to keep her in place. At least then, she did not have to view his disapproving frown. He had proved proficient in the saddle, cantering the entire way and reining with only one hand, but she could hardly compliment him—he looked in no mood for flattery.

They entered Arden Hall through a massive wooden door, which led into a great expanse of marble floor and potted plants. A butler stood ready, his frown deeper than his master's.

"Fetch my mother, will you, Naughton?"

His butler did as he was bid.

Lucinda's relief that his mother resided with him was short-lived. What would his mother do once she knew who she was? Mrs. Darrow, the wife of Alaric's nephew and heir, had said the entire village near Ivy Park was curious about their nuptials. It had been quite a surprise that Alaric had wed. Lord Grafton's mother would have heard all the gossip and more. Was she as much of a stickler for propriety as her son?

"Can you stand?" Lord Grafton asked as they waited for his mother.

"Yes." She would crawl if she had to. Anything was better than remaining in his unyielding arms. He carried her as if she were something scraped off the road.

He let her down.

She stood as poised as possible with her damp skirt and pelisse hanging lifeless about her legs and bedraggled hair falling past her shoulders. Her trembling started again and she held her arms in an attempt to keep in the warmth given from Lord Grafton's body. She needed a hot bath.

After only moments, a woman of uncertain years hurried toward her, her caring gaze not at all haughty. "My word, Dougie, what happened?"

"This is Lady Darrow. There has been a carriage accident and Sir Alaric was killed. I must return for his body. Can you manage?"

His mother waved him away. "Go on." Then she draped a comforting arm around Lucinda's shaking shoulders. "Come, my dear. How awful for you. Can you walk up the stairs, do you think?"

"Yes." Lucinda finally relaxed.

Lady Grafton issued orders to the housekeeper to ready a hot bath in the blue room and to make tea.

Lucinda gratefully leaned into the elder woman as they made their way up the stairs. "I am Sir Alaric's wife," she said to make sure things were clear.

"Yes, I know. I knew he planned to marry. We received your invitation. My apologies for not attending." Lady Grafton was clearly moved by Lucinda's young age and she treated her with kindness.

"But then you would be there instead of here," Lucinda mumbled. She was so tired she hardly made sense.

"You poor thing." Lady Grafton gave her a quick squeeze. "I am so sorry to hear about Sir Alaric. We will get you warm in no time and if you wish you may tell me all about it."

"Thank you, Lady Grafton."

*   *   *

Grafton and his groomsman arrived at the over-turned carriage just as the sun dropped below the heavy gray clouds. "We'll have to come back for the carriage in the morning. Let's get the body on the wagon."

Once inside the carriage, Grafton was shocked to find the contents completely stripped. No picnic basket, no deerskin rug, and even Grafton's black greatcoat, which he had left under Sir Alaric's head, had been taken. Grafton clenched his hands into fists.

Who would be so cold as to rob a dead man? Or was it all part of the plan to hide the poison? But he had the flask. He would turn it over to the apothecary to analyze its contents. He would get to the bottom of who was responsible for Sir Alaric's death.

With the help of his men, he loaded the wagon with the few pieces of luggage that had been left untouched. Then they pulled Darrow's body out of the carriage and loaded it on the wagon. They covered it with canvas and headed for Ivy Park, where they would leave Sir Alarics's body with the housekeeper and send word to the man's family.

By the time Grafton returned, chilled through from the rain and looking forward to a soak in the tub, his mother was waiting for him.

"How did Mrs. Lamb take the news?" his mother asked.

Sir Alaric's housekeeper had remained calm, but he could tell she was devastated. "As well as one might expect under the circumstances."

"Of course." His mother looked thoughtful, then added, "Our guest is an exhausted young woman."

"Should we send for a physician?"

"No. She is fast asleep. Her eyes closed before she had finished her tea."

Grafton nodded. The vulnerable picture his mother had conjured up before him battled with his own vision of the determined fortune hunter that was Lucinda Bronwell. Could she have poisoned Sir Alaric? If so, would a woman who had killed her husband on their wedding day sleep soundly?

"What happened, Dougie? Lady Darrow seemed afraid, even of me. It is downright shameful that Alaric married a girl so young."

"Do not let that *girl* fool you, Mother. She is a brazen fortune hunter who manipulated Sir Alaric into marriage. She knew exactly what she was about."

"Alaric dodged the parson's mousetrap for years. I cannot believe that girl led Sir Alaric anywhere he did not wish to go. Does she have family that we should alert?"

"In the morning, Mother. It will keep until the morrow." He stretched. "For now, I am in need of a hot bath." He kissed the top of his mother's head and bounded up the stairs.

Soon he sat soaking in his copper tub filled with hot soapy water and realized he would need from the local apothecary more than a simple statement that the contents of Sir Alaric's flask were indeed poison before the magistrate would act. Names of suspects would have to be supplied to the local constable in order for the magistrate to open his court. Which meant Grafton needed more proof before simply handing Lucinda over to a constable whose fairness was questionable at best. She might or might not have had a hand in her husband's death.

He let out a sigh. He had promised Sir Alaric he would protect her. The fear in the old man's eyes on her behalf had been very real. Whoever wanted his neighbor dead might also wish the same for his young widow.

The following morning, Lucinda woke with a nasty headache and a dry mouth. Her stomach lurched in protest to the sweet smell of chocolate, which had been left by a servant on her bedside table. She needed something bland like toast.

She sat up and rubbed her eyes. Her trunks lay open and emptied. Feeling dizzy, she carefully rose from her bed and stepped into a dressing area. Her clothes had been pressed and hung with care. She must have slept through the servants' flurry of unpacking, because she did not recall any of it.

Quickly she washed herself and donned a fresh dress. She checked her image in the cheval mirror, making sure her hair was neat and her gown respectable. Lord Grafton's critical gaze made her feel like a fishwife. She did not wish to appear anything less than a lady.

She headed out of her bedchamber to the stairs. Lord Grafton's home was indeed large. She lost her way a couple of times, until a maid gave her directions to the breakfast room. She badly needed to eat.

She noticed how sunshine streamed through the tall windows on either side of the front door, casting rainbows upon the marble tile. Distracted, she watched the colors dance and shimmer, wishing that the day before had not happened, that it was all a terrible dream.

She swallowed the urge to cry and made her way to the cozy room used for the morning meal. Gently, she pushed open the door and her heart dropped. Lord Grafton lingered at the table. She thought to retreat but it was too late. He looked up and saw her.

"Good morning, Lady Darrow. Do come in and break your fast."

"Thank you."

He rose as she took a seat. "Might I fill your plate?"

"Please. Toast, I think." She opened the folded napkin and placed it upon her lap. She noticed that pots of coffee and tea had been placed in the middle of the table with cups and milk and sugar. She helped herself to the tea.

"Sleep well?" He set a steaming plate of buttered eggs and sliced ham with toast before her, then returned to his seat.

Her stomach rumbled in response to delicious-smelling food. Perhaps she was hungrier than she had thought. "I slept very well, thank you," she said without looking at him. Taking small bites, she concentrated on her food, waiting for any adverse reactions from her abused belly. She experienced nothing more than the grumbling pangs of hunger.

"Amazing how the body shuts down after such tragedy," Lord Grafton said sarcastically.

"Amazing." She did not care one whit for his tone.

"Do you not wish to know what I have done with your husband's body?"

Lucinda finally looked at him. His dark hair was

in need of a trim and it curled along his shirt collar. She bit back an insolent retort and remained silent. He would no doubt tell her what she needed to know.

"He rests at Ivy Park. A message was dispatched to Sir Alaric's nephew straightaway."

She had not thought of alerting anyone. She could hardly remain upright when she arrived yesterday, let alone think. She owed him some measure of gratitude for handling the situation. "Thank you. I will need to make my mother aware of my circumstance."

He went on as if he had not heard her. "The contents of the carriage, including the picnic basket, were gone when we arrived, but your luggage had not been touched."

"Again, I thank you for taking such care in unpacking my things but that was not necessary."

He inclined his head. "Of course we had to search your bags."

She dropped her fork with a clatter against her plate and raised her chin. "For what, pray tell? Lord Grafton, I did not poison my husband."

His gaze narrowed. He looked taken aback by the firmness of her response. "You must understand that I will find out who did."

If he thought he could intimidate her, he was wrong. She had suffered any number of humiliations the past two years of her life and would no doubt be subjected to even more now that Sir Alaric was dead, but she was not about to stand for his arrogant implications that she would do away with her husband.

She squared her shoulders and looked him straight

in the eyes. "I hope that you do. In fact, I will help you in every way that I can, but for now, I wish only to go home."

"I cannot allow that," he said softly.

Anger fused through her, warming her cheeks and making her head pound even harder. "Cannot or will not?"

"I swore an oath to protect you and I cannot very well meet my obligation should you leave. Of course, if you insist, I can turn over what I know to the local constable. I planned on paying a visit to the apothecary and county magistrate this morning. Perhaps you would join me and explain to him why you could not possibly be responsible for what happened."

Her eyes widened and her mind raced to grasp her situation clearly. She was completely at his mercy. She did not wish to put her family through interrogations. Her mother would not fair well under the strain. "Very well. I shall remain under your protection but only if you send for my mother." Her chin trembled and her anger dissolved. She felt alone. Even so, she was not about to breakdown in front of him. "I need mourning clothes and she can bring them to me."

His gaze softened somewhat. "That can be arranged. Perhaps after you have eaten, you might join me in my study. I believe a letter to Sir Alaric's solicitor informing him of the circumstances of your husband's demise might be wise."

She wiped her mouth with a napkin and stood.

"When you are finished." He gestured for her not to rush.

"I am finished, Lord Grafton. I have completely lost my appetite."

She felt some pleasure at seeing his haughty expression wiped away. For a moment, he looked as if he regretted his terse manner, but then she might have been mistaken. His expression once again one of polite blankness, he stood. "Then let us make haste."

She followed him down the lengthy hallway to his study, her head pounding in earnest and her thoughts reeling. Her fate rested in the hands of a man who loathed her. Why did this have to happen? Finally, when she thought she had everything under control, disaster struck.

They entered the study, where a fire had been laid in the grate, filling the room with cozy warmth that wrapped itself around her. His large desk was scattered with stacks of papers and ledgers. A spot of wet ink lay on a piece of parchment as if he had been working here earlier. Checking the clock upon the wall behind his desk, she saw the hour read half past nine o'clock. Lord Grafton was not one to laze abed all morning.

"Are you familiar with the offices Sir Alaric uses in London?" He sat in a leather chair.

"I am. Mr. Spenlow is his solicitor. My mother and I met with him on several occasions."

He raised an elegantly arched dark brow. "Very well. Here is paper and quill. If you would grant Spenlow permission to discuss the matters of Sir Alaric's will and estate with my solicitor, Robert Sinclair, we may find suspects to look toward."

Lucinda nodded, relieved that Lord Grafton was willing to look for other possible culprits responsible for the crime. She knew he had connections and planned to use them.

Mr. Spenlow was an honest man. Sir Alaric had praised him highly for his services. He had settled her father's debts quickly and treated her family with the utmost respect. That carried much weight with Lucinda. She longed to be treated thus by all, but knew better than to expect the impossible. She was a fortune hunter after all.

She finished the letter and signed her name. Then she handed it to Lord Grafton for him to read.

Again he raised his eyebrow, much to her irritation. She took another blank sheet of parchment to compose a letter to her mother. After all her family had been through, she was not about to put them under the nose of an inept constable who would haul them before an unethical magistrate. For all she knew, the constable was in Lord Grafton's pocket or the killer's.

How easy it would be to pay the local authorities to cast all guilt her way. She did not stand a chance considering the circumstances of her marriage. Lord Grafton must know that. As much as she regretted the idea, she needed Lord Grafton's protection.

Writing the letter to her mother was much more difficult. How could she possibly explain what had happened with mere words? She chose discretion.

Dear Mama,
    There has been a carriage accident and Sir Alaric, the poor soul, was killed. I am currently at Arden

Hall under the protection of Lord Grafton and his mother. Please come quickly and bring the blacks I wore after Father's death.

Sorrowfully,
Lucinda

She handed over that letter as well. If Lord Grafton hurried with his dispatch, her mother might arrive by nightfall.

He read her last letter quickly. "Very good," he said as he folded the parchment. "I shall send my carriage for her straightaway." He sealed her letters with wax. Tucking them into his waistcoat pocket, he looked at her with all seriousness. "I believe it wise to keep the circumstances of Alaric's poisoning quiet until we know more from the solicitors. It is news best kept between you and me."

"I understand." Although she did not truly, it was one less problem she would have to lay at her mother's feet. "Bronley Manor is south of Banbury but north of Oxford," she said.

"My coachman will know the way."

Perhaps if she was her most amiable, he would be swayed to believe in her innocence. It certainly was worth a try. She briefly touched his arm and looked up into his face. "Thank you."

His expression was veiled, as if he weighed what game she played, but finally he nodded. "You are welcome." He pulled the bell rope and in no time a servant appeared to do his bidding.

"What of Lady Grafton? Will your mother mind?" Lucinda asked as she rose to leave.

This earned an actual smile from the young earl.

"To the contrary. She will enjoy the company immensely."

Lucinda nodded, relieved. Perhaps this arrangement would turn out to be tolerable.

Chapter Three

*G*rafton sent his carriage to Bronley Manor to fetch Mrs. Bronwell as promised. Letters to the solicitors had also been sent. He invited his solicitor, a boyhood friend, to come to Arden Hall that they might go over the list of beneficiaries for Sir Alaric's will in person. All he could do now was wait, and attend to his own affairs.

As he sat behind his desk with a slew of ledgers before him, his mind continually wandered to Lucinda's reactions this morning. The way her blue eyes widened innocently. She did not grow demure upon his implications but faced them head-on. Her denial rang true to his ears, but could he be sure? He had acted the brute not without purpose. He did not trust Lucinda Bronwell.

Her performance when they had first met in London was at odds with the woman he had rescued yesterday. He wondered if perhaps she created whatever demeanor she believed the situation called for. Her indignant anger might very well be an act.

He supposed only time would tell. As morning

turned into afternoon, Grafton received news from a servant that Lucinda had remained in her room. He decided he had best have a conversation with his mother. He was getting very little work done. With a sigh, he pulled the bell rope to call a servant.

A footman entered his study moments later. "Sir?"

"Is my mother at home?"

"Indeed, sir. She is having tea in her rooms."

"Very well. Please let her know that I shall be with her directly."

The footman bowed and left.

Grafton tidied his ledgers, knowing he would not get back to them anytime soon, and headed for his mother's sitting room. He opened the door quietly and found his mother lounging near the fire, a book in one hand, her brow furrowed.

She was a voracious reader and far too intelligent for her own good. She questioned any mystery she encountered, especially her son's failure to find a bride this past spring in London.

Grafton spied an open box of chocolates, with several pieces missing, on the divan next to her. "You will ruin your figure if you eat many more of those."

She looked up, and her gray eyes brightened. He had inherited his height from his mother, along with her perfectly chiseled features. Her hair, though graying, still shone a luxuriously dark shade of brown.

"As if I care." She marked her place in her book and scooted to a more upright position, moving the chocolates to a side table. "What is on your mind, Dougie?"

"I have sent for Lady Darrow's mother, Mrs. Bronwell."

"Good."

"They will no doubt be with us until Sir Alaric's funeral. In fact, I prefer that they remain here."

"Fine. I shall have another room made ready." His mother's gaze bore into him. "Something else troubles you."

He was not ready to spill all that had happened to Sir Alaric to his mother. In due time, when he had more answers than questions, he would enlighten her. "Not at all. I simply have much to do in closing out the end of this month's accounts."

"And our guest is a distraction."

"You might say that, yes."

"She is quite lovely. A more beautiful creature I have yet to see."

He held his breath. He knew where this was going.

"Come now, Dougie, do not say you have not noticed her looks." His mother popped another chocolate into her mouth and offered the box to him.

He grabbed one. "I'd be a dead man if I didn't. But she is completely unacceptable in every way. You may stop your mind from churning." He bit into the bittersweet dark chocolate.

"You are too picky by half, my dear, and you will grow old and die before you find the epitome of whatever it is you are looking for in a lady."

"Mother, please." He swallowed the rest of his chocolate. "Respectability and fine manners are not so tall an order. Lucinda Bronwell, now Lady Darrow, is the farthest distance from both. Besides, she's been widowed less than a day!"

"It could not have been a love match, Dougie, and you know it."

He snorted his contempt. He was not so hard to please, really. He wanted a virtuous bride in whom he could take pride—a woman highly regarded among his peers. Lucinda Bronwell simply did not meet that standard.

His mother ignored him. "The least you could do is keep an open mind."

He nearly laughed. His mother, who rarely went to Town, did not know the way things were done. She and her two dearest friends, the vicar's maiden sister and an eccentric artist of noble birth, met regularly to discuss whichever book they had each agreed to read. The three of them tended to have wildly romantic notions where he was concerned. They had pushed several young ladies his way over the years.

He sighed. "Very well." He'd keep his mind, eyes, and ears open where Lucinda was concerned.

A knock, followed by Naughton entering the room, thankfully interrupted the conversation from going any further.

"Yes?" Grafton stood.

"Mr. and Mrs. Darrow here to see you, my lord." The butler's nose lifted. Naughton was more of a stickler for social standing than any of the patronesses of Almack's. He obviously felt Grafton's late neighbor's relations beneath interest.

But Grafton felt otherwise. He was glad they had come so quickly. "Show them to the drawing room and have Mrs. Smith bring tea. And do fetch Lady Darrow to join us if she is well."

"Very good, sir."

"You are welcome to join us," Grafton said to his mother.

"Very well. I suppose it is time that I dressed."

Grafton wasted no time. He nodded, then headed down the hall. He very much looked forward to meeting Sir Alaric's heir.

Lucinda's heart stopped when a maid informed her that Sir Alaric's nephew and his wife were waiting in the drawing room. She paced the floor of her bedchamber, fretfully chewing her bottom lip.

If Lord Grafton believed her capable of such treachery against her husband, what would Mr. and Mrs. Darrow think? Mrs. Darrow had never approved of the match. She had never said so, not in words at least, but Lucinda knew—she could tell.

Sylvia Darrow, a woman not much older than she, had grudgingly hosted their wedding at her husband's lovely old manor near Coventry. Mr. Darrow had not been concerned with anything more than refills of his brandy.

Lucinda quickly changed into an afternoon dress with the help of the maid sent to fetch her. Together they rearranged her hair into a fashionable upsweep. Armed with the string of pearls given to her by Alaric, Lucinda took a deep breath. She was grateful for the large meal she had eaten at midday. Nourishment had greatly improved her constitution, as had a long nap.

Taking a deep breath, she followed the maid. When she entered the drawing room, Lord Grafton politely rose to his feet.

"Lady Darrow, how good of you to join us." His face was grim.

Lucinda bowed to all. Had she kept them waiting too long?

Mrs. Darrow also stood with her hands outstretched. "My dear Lucinda, how awful, simply horrible. You poor dear."

Lucinda briefly took the woman's hands. "Thank you, Mrs. Darrow."

"Come now." She flashed an uneasy look at Lord Grafton. "No need to stand on ceremony, my dear. We are, after all, family. You must call me Sylvia."

Lucinda nodded in spite of her reluctance. She had never before dared use Mrs. Darrow's Christian name. Family, indeed! The woman referred to her own husband as Mr. Darrow.

Mrs. Darrow pulled Lucinda to sit down next to her on the settee. "I was just telling Lord Grafton that we have settled in at Ivy Park. Our things will arrive later this week, but you must come and stay with us until everything is sorted out."

Lucinda glanced at Lord Grafton for help. He had been terribly silent.

"I'm afraid that is not possible," Lord Grafton drawled.

Mrs. Darrow cocked her head to the side. "Pray, why not?"

Lucinda nervously awaited Lord Grafton's answer. She clenched her hands into fists as they lay in her lap, to keep them still. What answer would he give?

"Lady Darrow is still recuperating from the accident and should not be moved until she regains her strength. Her mother joins her this evening."

"Oh, yes, I see. Of course, we cannot have Lucinda suffer a relapse, can we, Mr. Darrow?" Mrs. Darrow elbowed her husband, who had dropped off into a snooze in the chair next to the settee.

"What's that, dear?" He looked bewildered.

At that moment, Lady Grafton entered, followed by Mrs. Smith, the housekeeper, with the tea cart. "Do forgive my tardiness. Mr. and Mrs. Darrow, good to see you both. Thank you for coming."

Mr. and Mrs. Darrow stood, as did Lord Grafton.

Lady Grafton waved them away. "Please sit down."

"I informed the Darrows that Lady Darrow would do better to remain at Arden Hall until she regained her strength."

Lady Grafton poured tea expertly and handed Mrs. Darrow a dish. "My goodness, yes. She was terribly bruised. I think she should not be moved so soon."

Lucinda was grateful for Lady Grafton's expressed opinion and she could only wonder if her entrance and agreement had been staged or planned beforehand. Regardless, her comments closed the subject completely.

"My deepest condolences," Lady Grafton said. "Your uncle's accident was a terrible shock."

Lucinda accepted a cup of tea from Lady Grafton and took a sip. Over the rim, Lucinda glimpsed worry in Mrs. Darrow's eyes, which was quickly masked with a sweet smile. "Thank you, milady. Mrs. Lamb, uncle's housekeeper"—Mrs. Darrow glanced at Lucinda—"she told us all about Sir Alaric's tragic crash and how Lord Grafton came upon the carriage. Mr. Darrow and I are indeed grateful."

Mr. Darrow nodded but remained silent. He looked a little lost.

"Will the services be held shortly, then?" Lucinda asked.

"There are many in the community who will wish to pay their respects, I am sure. We have contacted Uncle's solicitor in London. We will know more when we hear back from him."

"Indeed." Lucinda's heart was heavy with regret. She should have been the one to oversee the tenants' paying of respects before the actual funeral. She was Alaric's wife. But then, his nephew was the new baronet. Perhaps she would not be welcome, considering who she was and the circumstances surrounding her marriage. She had never before seen Alaric's country home. She was a complete stranger to Ivy Park.

Grafton accepted a cup of tea from his mother with a nod. "I shall personally escort Lady Darrow to the funeral." He had watched the exchange between Lucinda and the Darrows very closely.

Lucinda had been pale and nervous when she entered the drawing room. Her color had not improved as the conversation wore on, but her nervousness stilled into something much worse. She looked grief-stricken. Her eyes were moist and occasionally her bottom lip trembled slightly as if she held her emotions in check.

Sitting next to the animated Mrs. Darrow on the settee, Lucinda looked terribly vulnerable. She made a sorrowful picture he hardly expected. He did not care for his urge to protect her, which had nothing to do with the oath he had pledged to Sir Alaric.

Something in him responded to her on an elemental level—a primitive instinct to vanquish her distress.

He did not care for the Darrows either. Mrs. Darrow seemed the money-hungry sort, too eager to please, and nervous besides. The nephew was exactly as Grafton had heard—a useless fellow who cared only for strong drink. His ruddy, bulbous nose and red-rimmed eyes were proof positive that the man had wasted himself on spirits.

When the Darrows finally took their leave, Grafton's mother walked them to the door, leaving him alone with Lucinda, who continued to sip her tea.

"That must be cold by now. Would you care for a warm-up?"

She glanced up at him, her large blue eyes troubled. "Yes, thank you."

"You do not rub along well with the Darrows." Grafton poured the tea, then added a lump of sugar and some milk.

" 'Tis more that they do not accept me, or at least Mrs. Darrow does not."

"They did not approve of Sir Alaric's choice in a bride?" He saw her wince.

"They did not approve of Sir Alaric marrying anyone, but I suppose I understand their reasons."

He arched a brow. He'd like to hear them, from her perspective at least. He handed her the tea.

She looked at him as if he should know what she meant. "Mr. Darrow is Alaric's heir. If there had been a child . . ." Her face colored to a bright red.

An unwanted vision of Lucinda carrying Sir Alaric's child flashed in Grafton's mind. The very thought of that lecher touching her disturbed him. "Mr. and Mrs. Darrow would have lost their position if you had had a son."

"Exactly." She sipped the steaming brew.

"It could hardly have anything to do with the fact your family was up to their eyeballs in debt and you are far too young for a man like Sir Alaric."

Her gaze flew to his. "He was a good man."

Grafton let out a snort of contempt. "Do we speak of the same Sir Alaric? He was an old roué who ran with my father's set!"

Lucinda set down her cup with a clink on the marble-top table. "He was all that was kind to me and my family." She stood up, ready to leave.

He had offended her. It was laughable to think that he could do such a thing to Lucinda Bronwell. "Why did it take six months for you two to wed?" He wondered if perhaps Sir Alaric had had second thoughts. Or had she?

She looked at her hands. "Alaric did not wish to press me. He thought it a good idea to know each other better. He spent considerable time at Bronley Manor with my family."

He had not expected that answer. It spoke well of Sir Alaric's motives. Lust had not been the primary consideration in his decision to offer for the luscious Lucinda. What then had Sir Alaric seen? After remaining a bachelor for so long, what had made him offer for a girl younger by forty years or more?

Grafton looked at her closely. She was indeed lovely, as his mother had so obviously pointed out, but she was more than simply a beautiful face. There was something deep and disquieting about her.

Lucinda looked up at him, her gaze holding his for a long while.

He finally looked away.

He cleared his throat and stood. "Your mother will no doubt arrive in time for dinner. You will wish to rest."

"Yes." She curtsied and took her leave.

Grafton watched her go. He looked forward to hearing from his solicitor. It had only been a day, but he considered Mr. and Mrs. Darrow suspects in Sir Alaric's death. As Lucinda had said, if she had borne a son, Mr. Darrow would have lost his place as heir to the baronetcy. Surely that was reason enough to deliver a picnic basket filled with death rather than good wishes.

Lucinda fretted about Lord Grafton's arrogant remarks, Alaric's funeral, and how to keep the truth about the poison from her mother without causing her worry. She had never hidden anything from her mother before.

A knock brought her head up from the book she was trying to read. Her bedchamber had been well stocked with popular novels and poetry.

"Come in."

The door opened and the concerned face of her beloved mother peeked into the room.

Lucinda was up in a trice. "Mama!"

Her mother rushed to envelop her in a hug. "Dearest Lucy."

Tears dripped from her eyes and her throat felt thick as she buried her face in her mother's sweetly scented shoulder.

"Hush now, my girl. 'Tis all right now." Her mother's voice soothed her like nothing else. "Tell me what happened."

Lucinda followed her to the bed, where they both sat upon the edge. "I can hardly believe it myself."

Her mother waited patiently. She had married at a very young age, and she bore Lucinda before a year had passed. Lucinda sometimes felt as though they were friends of a similar age rather than mother and daughter. Many had mistaken them for sisters— until her father's death had aged her mother with worry and grief.

Her father's death, a mere three years ago, had hit their family very hard. Her mother had been so devastated that she had fallen into a deep decline. Just when they had finally pulled each other through the darkness of sorrow, her father's debts surfaced with demands of payment that could be put off no longer.

They had sold everything they could to keep their creditors at bay until Lucinda was old enough to enter the marriage mart. With the help of her aunt in Town, Lucinda shook off all romantic notions of love and went to work attracting the attentions of wealthy gentlemen any way she could during her Season.

Lucinda grabbed a pillow and worried the edges. "Sir Alaric and I were in a carriage accident on our way to the Rose and Slipper Inn. I saw him die."

Her mother touched her fingers to still them from fidgeting. She asked, "Lucinda, what happened?"

"I do not know. One moment we were traveling along, and the next, the carriage tumbled over and over and Sir Alaric was mortally injured."

Her mother's hand flew to her chest. "Terrible, monstrous—oh, Lucinda." She reached out her arms.

Lucinda collapsed into her mother's embrace once again. "Lord Grafton came upon the wreckage. He brought me here."

"We owe Lord Grafton our gratitude."

Lucinda eyes felt heavy. "Indeed we do." She wished he did not look at her as if she were lower than dirt. And she wished more than ever she did not have to endure Mrs. Darrow's insincere kindness, the funeral, or facing Àlaric's tenants and servants and reading the suspicion in their eyes. All she wanted was to go home. But Lord Grafton had made himself perfectly clear. He wouldn't allow it.

Dinner had been held back to allow Mrs. Bronwell a chance to settle in and visit with her daughter. Grafton's stomach rumbled in protest. He was used to a schedule.

He sat behind his desk in his study, deep in thought. He had gone into the village and visited with the apothecary. The remaining liquid in the silver flask had enormous traces of arsenic. When he had described how painfully Sir Alaric had died, the apothecary—trained in London—immediately knew that Sir Alaric had ingested a large concentrated quantity of the poison for it to work so quickly.

Grafton thought about Lucinda and the small *sip* she had taken. Had she purposely drunk a minuscule amount?

If she had been the one to poison her husband, that still did not account for the theft of Sir Alaric's belongings. The thieves had not touched the luggage that contained valuable jewelry. Instead, they had taken only a worthless picnic basket and the valuables on Sir Alaric's person. If they were not part of the murderous scheme, then they were inept footpads.

Grafton raked a hand through his hair. There was nothing to do until he knew more. In the meantime, he looked forward to meeting Mrs. Bronwell, who had arrived while he had been out. Surely that woman would hold some clues to Lucinda Bronwell's true person.

He darted up the stairs to his bedchamber and rushed his toilette. Dressed in evening clothes of a black jacket and trousers, he surveyed his image in the mirror. He was never one to wear jewels, but tonight he decided to don a square topaz stickpin in the folds of his cravat just to gauge Lucinda's reaction. If she truly were money-hungry, she would no doubt notice the pin as something of great value.

Soon after joining his mother in the drawing room to wait with their guests for dinner to be announced, Grafton looked up to see Lucinda enter next to a woman so similar in appearance that she could only be her mother. Mrs. Bronwell was demure in demeanor and dress. She wore a modest evening gown made from the finest gray silk. Her blond hair was not nearly as brilliant in hue as her daughter's as it was liberally streaked with gray. Although she was much more fragile looking than her daughter,

Grafton could easily see where Lucinda had received her beauty.

He bowed deeply over her hand. "You must be Mrs. Bronwell. Welcome."

"I owe you my deepest gratitude, Lord Grafton, for coming to my daughter's aid." Her voice was soft and refined. There was no trace of groveling poverty or coarseness in her. Her manners bespoke a woman of breeding and she carried herself as such.

"You are most welcome," he said.

"You and Lady Grafton have been most kind in opening your home while Lucinda recuperates from the accident and awaits Sir Alaric's funeral. We are in your debt," Mrs. Bronwell said.

"Please." His mother waved away the compliment. "Think nothing of it. Dougie enjoys the role of knight-errant."

Grafton wondered what Lucinda had told her mother. He looked at her and she shook her head slightly. She had not told her mother anything about the poison, and he relaxed.

He noticed that Lucinda dressed in full mourning blacks and he had to admit that the color suited her. The cut was extremely modest, and he surmised that these must be the gowns she had worn after her father had died. Her golden blond hair shone in the firelight and her large blue eyes looked dark and mysterious. A simple string of pearls, the same she wore this afternoon, adorned her neck. She did not appear impressed with his pin. In fact, she barely looked his way.

Lucinda was relieved when dinner was finally announced. Her mother and Lady Grafton seemed to get on rather well, leaving her to speak with Lord Grafton, only she had nothing to say to him. He watched her closely as if judging her every action and reaction. It grew exceedingly tiresome.

"Lady Darrow." He offered her his arm.

"Thank you." She walked with him along the length of hallway to the dining room.

They were seated at a long table—Lord Grafton at one end, Lady Grafton the other. Her mother sat across from her. The distance between them kept any intimate conversation at bay, but Lady Grafton kept up a flow of casual chatter that carried them all through a formal meal of five courses.

"I suppose we can leave Dougie to his port," Lady Grafton said when they had finished with the nuts and cheese. "Come ladies, the drawing room is definitely more cozy than this huge dining room."

Lucinda followed her hostess out, but not before catching Lord Grafton's gaze. His brow was heavy with concern. No doubt the responsibility of her care and the task of finding Alaric's killer weighed heavily upon his shoulders. Even so, she was glad to quit the room and leave his unnerving presence.

In the drawing room, Lucinda sat in a comfortable chair near the fire. Her mother and Lady Grafton played a quiet game of cribbage and Lucinda pulled the book she had been reading from her deep pocket and relaxed.

Unfortunately, it was not long before Lord Grafton joined them. His mother looked surprised at his appearance but said nothing and continued with her game. Lord Grafton sat down in the chair next to her.

"I hope you are feeling well," he said.

"Much better than yesterday, I assure you."

"Good." He leaned closer and whispered, "Because the flask contained a considerable amount of arsenic. Had you drunk more than merely a sip . . ."

Her eyes closed with a mixture of sorrow and dreadful relief that she had not swallowed more from her own flask. And then it dawned on her. "Lord Grafton, there were two flasks."

"How's that?"

"Alaric and I each had our own. There were two flasks in the basket. Alaric took one and handed the other to me."

"You are certain?"

"I am."

"It was not in the carriage when I returned for the body. The basket had been taken as well."

"But why?"

He looked deadly serious, but kept his voice low. "To cover their tracks."

Chapter Four

*T*hree days passed before the funeral was held in order to allow all parties listed in Sir Alaric's Will to be notified and arrangements made for their attendance.

Mr. Spenlow, Sir Alaric's solicitor, had kept Lucinda informed of the upcoming events. He had forwarded a list of those invited to the reading of Sir Alaric's last will and testament to Lord Grafton's solicitor as requested.

Ivy Park along with the title had transferred smoothly to Alaric's nephew. Mr. Darrow would now be called Sir Leonard and his wife, Lady Darrow. The bereaved relatives were firmly ensconced at Ivy Park and they were making a house party of the funeral.

The day after Sir Alaric's death, the church bells had rung in his honor and then nine times every day since. The funeral would put an end to that ritual but not before everyone knew who had died and had come to pay their respects accordingly.

Twice Sir Leonard and Lady Darrow had visited

Lucinda at Arden Hall. Each time had been more nerve-racking than the last as Lucinda was forced to graciously decline their repeated invitations of hospitality. She felt guilty and remiss in her duties as the *Dowager Lady Darrow*, but she certainly did not wish to be under their roof.

Lord Grafton remained adamant in his role as her protector. After the last visit, Lord Grafton had whispered close to her ear that he did not trust the Darrows as far as he could throw them and she had heartily agreed. Even so, his comment had surprised her. She was shocked that he had moved close to her willingly, and then he had delivered his caustic remark with a trace of humor that Lucinda had not realized he possessed.

As she thought more on it, she wondered if they were both overreacting. Surely no one meant her harm. Lord Grafton simply felt honor bound to the promise she had overheard him make to Alaric—to protect her and keep her safe. But then again, there had been two flasks of poison, which clearly meant that whoever was responsible for killing her husband did not care a whit if she had been harmed as well. That thought brought her no comfort.

Lucinda, dressed in full mourning blacks, sat silently beside her mother in Lord Grafton's carriage on their way to Ivy Park. He and his mother sat opposite and no one spoke—each wrapped up in morbid thoughts of deaths and funerals remembered. The day was perfect for the somber occasion. The sky was a dull gray with cold winds out of the north whipping through the trees.

Lucinda stared out the window in order to catch

her first glimpse of the estate she might have called home. They came around a corner and she saw a lovely stone building shrouded in mist. Ivy Park was a romantic heap of an estate covered with ivy and surrounded by rosebushes that had gone to hips.

Black crepe hung from the front door and every curtain had been drawn. Sadness caught in her throat. Had things been different, she would have been mistress here. And then she felt guilty once again at the relief that hung on the heels of her grief. She had not wanted this marriage for anything more than what it meant for her family.

As they pulled up the drive, her nerves fluttered with fear. Like a moth flying too close to the fire, Lucinda knew the next few hours would burn like nothing else she had ever experienced. The last few days at Arden Hall had insulated her from the reality of Alaric's death, and now it all but crashed in around her, making her tremble. Her husband had been murdered and one of the guests attending the funeral might very well be responsible.

Grafton stood apart from the mourners paying their last respects to Sir Alaric Darrow before he was laid in the cold ground. Lucinda had amazed him yet again. She was as withdrawn and silent as one who genuinely grieved.

He watched her struggle with her composure as servants, tenants, and the local gentry approached her with their condolences. Some were hesitant toward her, and Grafton did not miss the whispers about her age and beauty, but regardless, Lucinda greeted them all with a soft smile and gentle words.

Many from London had gathered for the funeral. Sir Leonard and his wife had a houseful. The new Lady Darrow buzzed about, hosting a grand affair with little respect for the solemnity of the occasion. The housekeeper darted to do her new mistress's bidding with a dour expression.

Sir Alaric's business partner bowed low over Lucinda's hand and introduced himself as Mr. Lewes. The man looked a little harried, as if he had rushed to arrive. It was for him that Sir Alaric's funeral had been held back.

"I cannot believe *she* is here," Grafton's mother whispered.

Grafton looked around. "Who?"

"Lady Willow."

Grafton spotted the elegant widow of middle years. It was well known that she had been Sir Alaric's mistress. His gaze sought Lucinda's. Did she know?

"Poor girl," his mother went on, nodding toward Lucinda. "She tries to be brave, but I think she is shaking in her slippers. You should hear what is being said about her. All these people whom I have known for ages, Dougie, they are positively heartless."

"What are they saying?" he asked quietly.

"That she is far too young and a fortune hunter with no scruples who most likely did old Alaric in."

"Perhaps true statements, Mother."

"Nonsense. Can they not see how she grieves?" His mother stared long and hard at him. "Surely you do not believe . . ."

He ignored her.

"Douglas, do not say so."

"I won't."

His mother let out a deep sigh. "There is much speculation about her arrival in our carriage."

Grafton had heard nothing of that sort. "Such as?"

"You two are of a much more agreeable age."

His mother's implication was clear. "With you in residence and Mrs. Bronwell, the arrangements are completely respectable."

"The arrangements are not in question," his mother whispered.

Grafton's ire rose. Lucinda was a widow of less than a week. For anyone to think he had designs upon her was absurd and completely inappropriate—all the more reason to find the murderer and let Lucinda be on her way. He did not relish being the topic of idle gossip. "I'd hardly dally with a widow."

"Not the mighty Douglas Arden." His mother's tone was too sarcastic for his liking.

He glared at her.

"No one would fault you for succumbing to her beauty."

"Please."

His mother continued. "But I think she truly cared for Sir Alaric. Perhaps she has no interest in you at all."

He agreed. Lucinda hardly looked at him. In fact, the last three days they had spoken less than a dozen words. Not that he wished it otherwise.

He also did not think Lucinda playacted her grief. Her brimming tears were wiped away quickly when she believed no one looked at her. She remained fixed next to the coffin, speaking only to those who approached her. Her delicate mother stood guard next to her daughter as if daring anyone to be unkind.

Grafton knew that the gentlewoman was relieved that her daughter was no longer married. The other day he had chanced upon a conversation Mrs. Bronwell had had with his mother. She had shamefully confessed to taking comfort in the fact that Lucinda had been saved from the marriage bed with Sir Alaric. Of course, Mrs. Bronwell had awkwardly retracted those words uttered quite accidentally, but his mother had eased her embarrassment with understanding.

He could not say that he blamed Mrs. Bronwell for expressing her feelings, but it caused him to think of the polite Mrs. Bronwell in a new light. She clearly loved her daughter. Could Mrs. Bronwell have had a hand in the arsenic-laced brandy? He highly doubted it. Why chance two flasks? No, it hardly made sense, but he did not discard the notion completely, no matter how ludicrous.

He hoped to get a clearer sense of the most likely culprit when the will was read.

Lucinda stood shivering at the Darrow family grave site. The damp winds cut through her layered clothing with a chill that reached her bones. Many of the mourners had taken to their homes, but the servants were loyal to their former master. Those whom Lady Darrow had not given duties to perform were allowed to join the funeral procession to the small cemetery.

She watched the expressions on each mourner's

face as Sir Alaric's coffin was lowered into the ground. She looked for any hint of guilt or gladness that might reveal the one who had poisoned him. Lady Darrow sniffed and blew her nose into her handkerchief. Her husband, Sir Leonard, watched in morose silence, his face grim. Lady Willow had tears running down her cheeks, and Sir Alaric's business partner, Mr. Lewes, looked bored.

Her gaze met Lord Grafton's and he gave her a polite nod. She had almost forgotten his presence. He stood very tall and forbidding in his dark greatcoat and felt beaver, lending propriety and polish to the entire affair. Lady Darrow was in alt to have an earl in her home. She looked at him as if he were a prized goose stuffed and ready for Christmas dinner.

Her mother stood close to her side and held her hand. "How are you holding up, dear?" Her voice was soft and low.

She gave her mother's hand a squeeze. "I am fine."

The vicar read the service and closed with a prayer for those Sir Alaric had left behind. That was her cue. Lucinda moved forward to toss the first shovelful of dirt upon the grave. She stood back and watched as others did the same until finally the burial service was complete.

Back at Ivy Park, the procession gathered for tea in the drawing room and waited. Lady Darrow poured and Lucinda helped by handing each guest a steaming cup. Sir Leonard helped himself to a decanter of brandy from the sideboard.

"There now, are we not a cozy bunch?" Lady Darrow took her place next to Sir Leonard, her hands folded in her lap. Her brow wrinkled with obvious anxiety no matter how hard she tried to appear uninterested in the reading.

Lucinda watched as Mr. Spenlow shuffled through papers. She still shivered and wished she had sat closer to the fire. It would no doubt be a long ordeal, one she wished she did not have to endure. Lord Grafton and Lady Grafton were still seated as well, and she wondered if the reading would be open to them.

Mr. Spenlow cleared his throat. "Very well. Let us proceed. I see that all are present that need to be. Lord Grafton and Lady Grafton, please, do stay."

Lucinda felt the tension in the room wind a bit tighter as every set of eyes turned toward her. What did they expect to see? Raising her chin high, she leaned closer to her mother, who sat next to her on the couch. Lucinda grabbed her hand and waited.

"I shall read Sir Alaric's last will and testament," Mr. Spenlow started. "As you know, provisions had been made for Sir Alaric's nephew and heir to inherit the baronetcy encompassing Ivy Park and the house in London and all its contents along with an annual allowance from investments connected to the estate of five thousand pounds per annum."

Lucinda watched Lady Darrow's face closely. She was clearly disappointed with the amount. She had expected more. Sir Leonard cursed softly, then drank deeply from his goblet.

Lucinda glanced at Lord Grafton, who studied the Darrows closely. He suddenly looked her way and their gazes met. What was he thinking? He gave her an encouraging nod and then he turned his attention back to Mr. Spenlow. She tried to listen, but her mind wandered amid the monotone drone of Mr. Spenlow's list of items left for each of Sir Leonard's two sisters and then what the servants had been left.

Lucinda's attention was captured when the names of the guests were mentioned. She watched their faces, trying to judge their reactions as their names were read along with their entitlements.

Lady Willow was restored the business shares from her late husband that had been signed over to Sir Alaric after the two men had dueled. The reason for the duel had been left unclear, but Lucinda wondered if it had not been because of the elegant woman herself. Alaric had mentioned that his past had not been without improprieties.

Mr. Lewes inherited the building and machinery used for the silk business in Birmingham. But when it came to matter of the remaining shares, Lucinda's ears rang at the mention of her own name.

" 'To my wife, Lucy, I leave my business shares, the sum of twenty thousand pounds that has been placed in trust for her benefit and use. The provision of three thousand pounds per annum until such time that she remarries. The marriage settlements shall remain in force until such time they have been exhausted.' "

Mr. Lewes' face had turned red and he shot to his feet. "I protest! No, I shall contest! What need and knowledge could this woman possibly have to be left the remaining shares to my business? Spenlow? What?"

Mr. Spenlow pushed his spectacles up the bridge of his nose. "It is quite clear that Sir Alaric wished her to have them. Shall I finish?"

Mr. Lewes glared at her. "You bewitched him! Those shares were promised to me by Sir Alaric himself should something happen to him! How did you manage to change his mind?" Now he leered at her.

Lucinda trembled. "Mr. Lewes, I had no idea of their existence. I do not want them."

Lord Grafton was also on his feet, and he placed his hand upon her shoulder. "Careful now. Do not be so ready to give away what you do not understand. Lewes, back off! This is neither the time nor place."

Mr. Lewes sat down.

Lady Darrow's eyes were wide and she flailed her handkerchief as if she had trouble catching her breath. Lady Willow was the only person who appeared unruffled by the outburst. She gave Lucinda an encouraging nod, but remained quiet otherwise.

Lucinda swallowed hard, taking some measure of comfort and strength from Lord Grafton's warm hand still resting upon her shoulder. He stood behind her like a sentinel at his post.

Mr. Spenlow read on to state that in the event of Lucinda's death, the remaining trust funds would be held for her brother, Thomas, until he reached the age of twenty-five. The shares would revert to Mr. Lewes. And if Lucinda passed before she had remarried, the three thousand pounds per annum would transfer to her mother, Mrs. Bronwell.

Lucinda was deeply touched by Alaric's generosity. Her family had been amply provided for—Thomas' future success and that of Bronley Manor were guaranteed.

When Mr. Spenlow finished, all was uncomfortably

quiet. Lucinda felt suspicious glances from everyone. What was worse, they looked from her to Lord Grafton behind her, narrowing their eyes. It was then that she realized she had covered Lord Grafton's hand resting on her shoulder with her own, and he had grasped it to give her comfort.

Mr. Lewes' accusation that she had somehow bewitched Sir Alaric had taken hold. And now they believed she had worked the same magic upon her host and protector, Lord Grafton. She read as much in their glaring looks.

Appalled and frightened, she felt his hand slip away from hers and her face heated with shame. Not because there was any truth to Mr. Lewes' charge, but because she had been foolish enough to provide them with fodder to use as proof of the gossip about her.

Mr. Lewes stood and addressed Mr. Spenlow. "You, sir, shall hear from my solicitor. I will indeed contest this will." He turned on his heel and without another word stormed from the room.

Lucinda remained seated, numb.

Her mother stood. "Come, dearest, we must get you back to Arden Hall so you can rest."

She looked up into her mother's eyes and her own filled with tears. "They all think—"

"Hush now." Her mother turned to Lord Grafton. "My daughter is not feeling well, my lord. Might we leave?"

Lord Grafton went into action, giving his regrets to Lady Darrow. "It has been a long day."

Lady Darrow's voice sounded drained, as if all her

hopes had been dashed. "Indeed it has. And a surprising one."

"Lord Grafton, a pleasure." Sir Leonard bowed.

"No need to show us out." Lord Grafton nodded to Mr. Spenlow. "If you need to speak with Sir Alaric's widow, do let me know. Good day."

As they left Ivy Park, Lucinda leaned on her mother and Lady Grafton gave a cluck of sympathy. Inside the carriage, Lucinda could hold back no longer. She broke down and sobbed on her mother's shoulder.

Grafton sat in his study, a cup of steaming tea next to him. Robbie, his solicitor, sent word that he had taken rooms at the Rose and Slipper Inn. He would arrive at Arden Hall any moment.

Lucinda Bronwell was now an heiress. Did Lewes' words have merit? Good God, the woman had been engaged for six months and Sir Alaric had given her a large portion of his wealth. Did she charm him into it and then kill him? It was entirely possible, but highly unlikely.

She was as scared as a wind-tossed leaf while she listened to her husband's last will and testament. She had clutched his hand as if holding on for dear life, and he had obliged her.

He took a sip of tea.

The thought that he had wanted to comfort Lucinda did not sit well with him. It had taken all his willpower to keep from chastising Mr. Lewes for his hateful outburst, but he had held his tongue knowing that should he come too strongly to Lucinda's defense, it would only make the gossips' whispers that much more plausible. Enough damage had been done when everyone saw that he and Lucinda had held hands.

But he had seen a side of Lucinda he did not realize existed. A funeral was hardly the place to judge a person's true character, or was it? Her reaction to Sir Alaric's will was not consistent with a person who knew what to expect. Her emotional breakdown in the carriage was proof enough of that. Good God, by the time they had reached Arden Hall, he had three weeping women to contend with.

A scratch at the door brought his head up. "Come."

"Master Sinclair to see you, my lord." Naughton delivered the calling card on a silver tray.

Grafton picked up the card belonging to his solicitor. "Send him in."

In moments, Robert Sinclair stepped into his study and Grafton extended his hand. "Robbie."

Robbie accepted the handshake with warmth. "I came as soon as I could."

Grafton had grown up with Robbie Sinclair. He was the son of a wealthy merchant from Birmingham. They had gone to Eton together and then to Oxford. Robbie was well on his way to becoming a barrister, but Grafton had persuaded him to act as his solicitor once he came into the title. Grafton had never cared for his father's lawyers, who were too timid to give strong advice to a peer.

Fortunately, Robbie was both honest and outspoken. "I have the list from Spenlow's offices," Robbie said. "What's this about Sir Alaric Darrow being murdered?"

"To the point as always." Grafton pulled the bell rope. "Tea or something stronger?"

"Tea is fine."

"Very well. Let me fill you in on the events at the reading of Sir Alaric's will." They discussed all that had been given until tea was served.

Robbie sat back with a sigh. "She's an heiress."

"Precisely," Grafton agreed. "And yet I do not think she knew."

"Do you suspect her of poisoning Sir Alaric?"

"How can I not, considering what I know of her?"

"What do you know then?" Robbie asked.

"She made no secret that she was on the hunt for a wealthy husband during the Season. She pushed herself forward in a most vulgar way."

"Just because she acted in less than a respectable way does not make her a murderess."

"Of course not. But considering the amount she inherited—she certainly had much to gain by Sir Alaric's death and she had the opportunity to do the deed." Grafton showed Robbie the flask. "The apothecary confirmed the contents were laced with arsenic."

"An easily obtained poison."

"Exactly."

"What can I do?" Robbie sipped his tea.

"I was hoping that you might look into checking the backgrounds of the Darrows, Mr. Lewes, and even Lady Willow—all who have inherited."

"And what of the widow Darrow? Shall I check into her family history as well?"

"Indeed, you must." Grafton wanted to be certain that Lucinda's story was indeed true. Although deep inside, he knew it was. He hardly wanted to trust his feelings as a sure method of proving innocence. "Be discreet. I do not want anyone wise to what I am doing."

Robbie inclined his head. "Of course. It will be like the old days, when we spied upon your papa."

Grafton shifted uncomfortably. He never regretted his actions, which had proved his father for the irresponsible reprobate that Grafton knew him to be. Grafton had been young and headstrong. He and his father had never seen eye to eye the few times his father deemed it necessary to visit Arden Hall.

Angry that his sire's indecent affairs were common knowledge among members of the *ton*, Grafton could not allow more scandal to touch his mother. She had done nothing to warrant such neglect and disregard.

Grafton had had his father followed and was able to intervene before his father could take part in a duel with a member of the royal family. Grafton swore an oath then and there that he would never bring shame upon the name of Grafton. He had earned the respect of many and he intended to keep it that way.

Chapter Five

*G*rafton washed and changed for dinner. He had encouraged Robbie to join them, but the blasted man refused with the excuse that he had to be up and out early the next morning. Robbie took his duties seriously, which was one more reason Grafton entrusted him with this delicate matter. Robbie and one of his hired men would hunt for information on the beneficiaries of Sir Alaric's will and then he would meet with Grafton again.

Dressed in dark blue superfine and buff trousers, Grafton charged down the stairs and nearly ran into Lucinda at the bottom.

"Lord Grafton."

He bowed. "Lady Darrow, forgive my haste. How are you this evening?"

"Much better, thank you." Her cheeks were pink and she looked the very picture of good health.

Of course, her tears must have dried as soon as it sunk in how enormously rich she was. "Perhaps you might honor me with a conversation after dinner."

A flicker of fear flashed in her eyes before she

schooled her expression into a polite smile. "I shall look forward to it, my lord."

She was very good at controlling her emotions. In fact, watching her just now was like catching someone in the act of pulling the curtains closed to keep out nosy intruders. "Come now, Lady Darrow, no need for falsehoods. I assure you I have only business to discuss."

She tilted her head and looked down her perfectly straight nose. "Of course."

He offered her his arm. "Shall I escort you to the drawing room?"

She hesitated slightly, then placed her hand upon his arm. "By all means."

They walked silently down the hallway. Did she fear him? Surely not, but she did not wish to be in his presence—that much was obvious, to him at least. She was dressed in an outdated evening gown of full mourning black and she wore pearls that she nervously fingered.

"Lovely necklace," he said.

"A gift from Alaric."

"Strange that he would not have showered you with diamonds and gemstones."

"I like pearls and Alaric thought they suited me."

Lucinda preferred plain pearls? Grafton could hardly believe it; they were modest gems. She looked demure this evening in the high-necked gown with a black lace fichu draped around her neck covering any hint of skin. She looked the complete opposite of her image in Town. She did not even act the same.

The indecorous Lucinda Bronwell of London made a practice of wearing near transparent gowns with indecently low bodices. This reserved young lady with sorrow etched in her eyes could hardly be one and the same. Perhaps her antics in London were merely a bid for attention. But that was difficult to believe since her beauty rivaled any Incomparable. Who was the real woman?

They finally reached the drawing room, where their mothers were waiting.

"My dear Lucinda." His mother rose to greet her. "How are you managing? Your mother is beside herself with worry and so am I."

Grafton let go of Lucinda.

Lucinda took his mother's hands into her own. "You are a dear for thinking of me, but do not worry. I am fine now. I had a long nap."

Grafton hung back. It had only been a few days, but already his mother doted on Lucinda. His mother was no idiot. She could judge a person well, with the exception of his father perhaps, but then they did not speak of him. In fact, he knew little about the circumstances that brought his parents together, other than it was a marriage of convenience—his mother possessing the funds his father wanted in a wife.

Naughton entered the drawing room. "Dinner awaits."

Grafton bowed low. "Ladies, after you."

Lucinda concentrated on chewing her food. She could barely stand Lord Grafton's haughty gaze. He was too much of a gentleman to come straight out and accuse her, but his carefully phrased questions and studious glances spoke volumes.

Everyone thought she had killed her husband! No, it was worse. She had bewitched him into handing over the majority of his wealth first. Even Lord Grafton was shocked to hear how much she had received. He had heard Mr. Lewes' accusation and said nothing.

Oh, but what could he have said in her defense? It was true, she *had* married for money, but Sir Alaric had provided for her family in the marriage settlements. There was no reason for her to seek or want more.

"Dougie," Lady Grafton said, "this pheasant is simply divine."

Lucinda glanced at Lord Grafton. His Christian name was no doubt Douglas and the nickname was an ill fit. Lord Grafton was a tall, handsome man with angular features and a haughty inclination, as if he were hewn from cold stone. But his eyes were a stormy gray, like his mother's, and they softened when he looked upon her. He treated his mother with utmost respect and affection.

"When did you shoot the pheasants, dear?" Lady Grafton asked.

"Yesterday, or the day before. I cannot remember," Lord Grafton replied.

"Delicious," Lady Grafton said.

"Indeed," Lucinda's mother agreed.

Lucinda imagined Lord Grafton to be quite the sportsman. She envied his ability to traipse about the countryside while she must stay holed up inside. It was not the thing for a grieving widow to be seen out of doors before the funeral. And even after, she could hardly go far.

"The weather has been fine, with the exception of today, of course," Lucinda said. It was obvious to her that the dinner conversation was stilted at best. Lord Grafton was not exactly a chatterbox. Nor was she. But then she knew Lord Grafton dissected everything she said for hidden meanings.

"Exceptionally fine weather for late November, I daresay," Lucinda's mother added.

Her mother's efforts to keep the conversation moving failed. The meal progressed with long stretches of silence interrupted only by polite but inane comments until finally the bowl of sweetmeats, nuts, and cheese was brought round. After a brief indulgence, the ladies stood to depart.

"Lady Darrow, would you care to remain?" Lord Grafton asked.

Lucinda turned to her mother. "Do you mind?"

"Not at all, dearest. I shall be in the drawing room with Lady Grafton." Her mother's concerned gaze darted from Lord Grafton back to her.

Lady Grafton merely raised her eyebrow, an expression of inquiry so similar to her son's.

Lucinda sat back down when their mothers left the dining room. She waited quietly for Lord Grafton to raise the topic weighing upon his mind.

He remained silent as the servants brought a decanter and two crystal goblets. "Port, Lady Darrow?"

"No, thank you." She held her hands tightly in her lap, fearing she might fidget. Breathing deeply to calm her nerves, she leveled what she hoped was a confident and steady gaze at her host.

He poured himself a small portion of the amber

liquid. "Perhaps you would be more comfortable in my study?"

"This location is fine, my lord."

He took a sip, his dark gray eyes watching her over the rim of the glass. "How does it feel to be an heiress?"

"How does it feel, my lord?"

"Come now, Lady Darrow. We met in London. I know you were seeking a wealthy man to wed. And so you have, and he left you a rich widow," he said quietly.

She knew it! Mr. Lewes' accusation *had* affected him. As if she had control of what her husband had willed her. "Alaric was a generous man."

"Far more generous than even you expected."

"Lord Grafton, please make your point. I had no idea before today that Alaric would provide for me and my family in such a manner." She stood up, suddenly furious. If he would not say it, she would oblige him. "I did not kill my husband, nor did I bewitch him or entice him to change his will before we were married."

Lord Grafton stood, looking contrite. "Forgive me." He bowed. "I did not mean to upset you, but you must understand that I cannot rest until I find the person responsible for poisoning Sir Alaric. I could hardly keep my word if I did not settle in my own mind that you are unable to carry out such a deed." He let out a sigh and held out his hand. "Please, will you stay?"

She wavered. Did he wish to judge her depth of feeling? Why did she care what he thought of her? She was a fortune hunter. She could not erase that, especially from the memory of the man who stood before her. Defeated, she sat back down.

"If we are to help each other, we must endeavor to trust one another." His voice was soft, coaxing.

"How do you propose we do that?"

"By being open and honest."

"I have nothing to hide." Her motives, her pride, and her shame had all been laid bare.

"May I ask why you married Sir Alaric? Other than the obvious, of course."

She shifted in her seat. "We were desperate. It was my second Season and still the right gentleman had not presented himself. My aunt sponsored my come-out. She instructed me in the ways of attracting a gentleman of means, but the entirely wrong sort beleaguered me. Until I met Sir Alaric. I think he took pity on me. My family was on the brink of losing Bronley Manor. The papers sat upon my father's desk waiting to be signed by my mother. I could not allow my father's legacy and my brother's inheritance to be sold."

"And so you sold yourself." His voice remained soft but disapproval shone from his eyes.

" 'Tis a woman's lot and nothing uncommon, but I was more fortunate than many. Alaric was patient and kind. He settled my father's debts and put everything back to rights as part of the marriage settlement. The fact that he befriended my family was something completely unexpected."

"I see."

"I wish the killer to be brought to justice more so than you. I cared for my husband, Lord Grafton. I will not lie and claim that I loved him the way a wife should love her husband, but I would have done everything in my power to make him happy."

Grafton listened carefully to her speech. Her forthright manner and the passion with which she delivered it gave credibility to her words. He believed her, or perhaps he simply wanted to believe her beseeching blue eyes. A man could gaze upon her perfect beauty as one might a finely crafted work of art. The texture of her skin was flawless gossamer and her straight nose led to bow-shaped lips ripe for kissing.

He shook off such thoughts. "Once again, forgive me for doubting you, Lady Darrow."

She shrugged as if it were no matter. "You were present during the reading of the will. Who do you think might be the guilty party?"

A loaded question. "Many gained from Sir Alaric's death."

"Except Mr. Lewes. Why would Alaric leave his shares to me? I have no knowledge of business matters. What should I do with them?"

Grafton chuckled. "He must have had his reasons. Keep them for now, at least. Perhaps Spenlow might shed some light on the matter." He took another sip of port. "Lady Willow inherited only what truly belonged to her."

"Who is she?" Lucinda asked.

Grafton sat straighter and coughed. What on earth should he tell her? Openness and honesty. He had asked as much from her. "Lord Willow and Sir Alaric were very good friends until the love they had for Lady Willow nearly ruined them both. Rumor has it that the men dueled not to the death, but rather to the loss of their businesses. Lord Willow lost, and with it his main source of income."

"How dreadful. I did not know," she whispered, her eyes wide. "When did this happen?"

"Nearly three years ago. Lord Willow went into a decline after the duel. He became sickly until he finally died a few months later."

"I did not realize Alaric had been so ruthless."

"Please forgive me for tarnishing your memory of him."

She looked at him calmly. "He had once alluded to his less than proper past, but I had no idea his dueling had been so recent."

"Which brings us to Sir Leonard and his wife. They stood to gain the most and yet Lady Darrow was quite rattled by your portion."

"I was as well," Lucinda conceded with a shy smile.

As he looked at her, his gut twisted oddly and he felt warm about the ears. "Indeed."

"What will you do?"

"Find out all that I can about each person who was present at the reading of Sir Alaric's will."

"What if someone completely different is responsible?"

"We have to start somewhere and the funeral guests appear to be the best choice we have."

"Yes, of course, you are quite correct." She stared at nothing in particular.

He realized that after such a day, she must be exhausted. "I need not keep you further, Lady Darrow. I appreciate your candor, and if there is anything that might make your stay at Arden Hall more pleasing, do tell me."

She bit her lip. "There is one thing."

"And what is that, madam?"

"I wonder, sir, if you have a mount suitable for a lady? I would benefit from exercise more strenuous than strolling your gardens."

"You enjoy riding?"

"Indeed, I do. At home, I rode often."

He found her interest pleasing, indeed. "I am happy to accommodate you, but we can discuss the matter more thoroughly on the morrow. In fact, I will give you a tour of my stables. But now, you must rest."

She smiled. "Thank you, Lord Grafton. Until tomorrow then." She rose to leave.

"Tomorrow." He stood and watched her depart, wondering why on earth he looked forward to tomorrow.

Lucinda leaned against the wall in the hallway and breathed deeply. It was not nearly as bad as she had feared. Lord Grafton was overbearing, to be sure, but there was kindness underneath his haughty exterior. And perhaps he finally believed her to be innocent.

She would need him to, for her mother could hardly stay much longer at Arden Hall. Her sisters had been left under the care of the vicar and his wife until her return. Lucinda longed to go home and put all of this behind her. Perhaps now he would let her.

Exhausted, she entered the drawing room to bid her mother and Lady Grafton a good evening; then she headed for her bedchamber. After her maid helped her out of her stiff bombazine gown, she fell into bed. But sleep would not come.

Her thoughts raced with the possibilities of who might have poisoned Alaric. Mr. Lewes or the Darrows seemed the most likely candidates to have done the deed. She hoped Lord Grafton gathered his information quickly. But then what would he do with it?

Perhaps he would turn the matter over to the constable then and let him investigate further. She would have to ask Lord Grafton about his plan on the morrow when she looked over his horseflesh.

She snuggled deeper beneath the coverlet. She looked forward to a brisk ride and she knew Lord Grafton would insist on joining her. And that might not be a bad thing at all.

Chapter Six

*L*ucinda woke with a start and wondered where she was. Rubbing her eyes, she realized she was not at home, but still installed at Arden Hall. With a sigh, she read the time. Eleven o'clock. The events of the previous day had taken their toll and she had slept well past the time to break her fast in the morning room.

A maid stepped into her bedchamber. "Good, you're awake, miss." She carried a tray laden with chocolate and a light repast.

Her mother followed the maid. "I ordered something for you to eat quickly since Sir Leonard's wife is downstairs."

"How long has she been here?" Lucinda took a drink of chocolate, then darted behind a screen to wash.

"She just arrived. Lord Grafton asked that I see if you felt up to meeting her."

"Whatever could she want?" Lucinda splashed water on her face to rinse off the soap. She hurriedly toweled off and slipped into a chemise before coming out from behind the screen. She motioned for the maid to help her dress.

"Something about papers for you to sign," her mother said.

Lucinda rolled her eyes. She did not wish to deal with Alaric's will today. She had hoped to go riding with Lord Grafton. Disappointment washed over her. There was nothing to be done but see Lady Darrow.

The maid and her mother helped her don a simple morning gown of dark gray broadcloth edged with blond lace. With her hair done in a simple knot, Lucinda took a quick bite of toast before she headed down the stairs, wondering why Lady Darrow chose to call so early.

She stepped into the sunlight-filled room and smiled. "Good morning. I beg your pardon for keeping you waiting."

Lord Grafton stood. Lady Darrow, looking worried, remained seated on the couch.

"My dear Lucinda," she said quickly, "I simply had to come and see how you were after such an upsetting day yesterday. And also to tell you that Mr. Spenlow has papers for you to sign. He can come to Arden Hall at your convenience, or you may come to Ivy Park." She took a breath. "Seemed silly to send a message when I could easily come myself and make sure you were well." She held out a box tied with ribbon. "I also wanted you to have these." Lady Darrow's hand trembled ever so slightly.

"Thank you, Lady Darrow." Lucinda took the box and unwound the ribbon to reveal linen handkerchiefs that had been embroidered with her initials: *LD*. Lucinda did not know what to say.

"The servants had them ready to present to you when Uncle Alaric brought you home, but since— I thought you should have them." She glanced at Lord Grafton.

Lucinda nodded. "How very thoughtful."

"Indeed," Lord Grafton added. "Perhaps the dowager and I might ride over this afternoon and she can meet with Mr. Spenlow and sign those papers."

Lady Darrow's eyes brightened, but then her brow furrowed. "Oh, but are you feeling up to it? You were so bruised after the accident, but it would make things much simpler if you could come."

Lucinda's eyes narrowed. How difficult was it for Mr. Spenlow to travel the five short miles that separated Ivy Park and Arden Hall? But she looked forward to a ride and if Lord Grafton offered to accompany her, she was not about to refuse. "I am much recovered and certain a short ride will improve my health with a dose of fresh air." She glanced quickly at Lord Grafton.

"Indeed," he said with a curt nod. "We shall make the trip then."

"Very good," Lady Darrow said. "Do come in time for tea at, shall we say, three o'clock? I will let Mr. Spenlow know when to expect you." She rose without so much as a glance and curtsied. "I must return to my guests. Until later then."

Lord Grafton walked Lady Darrow to the drawing room door.

After she left, Lucinda sat down upon the couch with a sigh, the boxed handkerchiefs still in her hands. She looked at Lord Grafton. "Was that not a bit odd?" She raised one of the embroidered linen squares from out of the box. "These hardly seemed so urgent as to require a personal visit."

"Why do you think I offered for us to ride over there and have a look?" said Lord Grafton.

Lucinda nodded. "Thank you, sir."

"You may rue those words once you are in the saddle. Lady Darrow was quite correct in asking if your bruises will trouble you."

"Forgive my pertness, but I am eager to quit your house for the outdoors. Any additional aches and pains will no doubt be eased by a hot bath."

She was awarded a brief smile. Lord Grafton was incredibly handsome when he smiled. Lucinda concluded that smiling was something his lordship need do more often and she would try to help where she could.

Although she did not care to face the guests at Ivy Park, she longed to be out of doors. She felt as one caged at Arden Hall despite the fact that it was three times the size of Bronley Manor. At home, she had always come and gone into the village as she pleased. Even after her father's death, there was much to be done, so she was not nearly as isolated as she was here.

Lord Grafton stood. "Meet me in the stables at two."

Lucinda nodded and watched him leave, his broad shoulders taking up nearly the entire entryway. She left the drawing room for her mother's room. Nuncheon would soon be served in the breakfast room and then she would meet Lord Grafton.

Two and a half hours later, Lucinda entered the stables. Dressed in the black riding habit that her mother thought to bring, she waited while the groom administered to her mount.

"I have chosen a well-trained but lively mare for you to ride." Lord Grafton had come up behind her, leading his fully saddled stallion by the reins.

She turned to face him. He seemed even taller in the close quarters of the stables. "What is her name?"

"Ariel."

The same dappled gray he rode the day of the accident stamped at the ground and snorted. The horse was eager to be off. Lucinda could tell prime blood when she saw it. Her father had never had a horse so fine. She reached out her hand. "May I?"

He gently pulled his mount forward. "Settle down, Horatio. The lady wishes to scratch your ears." The softly spoken command stilled the stallion.

"He is lovely," Lucinda whispered. She ran her fingers down Horatio's nose and the stallion lifted his head proudly.

"Now he's showing off," Lord Grafton said.

"As well he should." Lucinda stepped back. "My father would have loved such a mount."

"Did he keep a stable, then?"

"A very adequate one, but we had none this prime."

Lord Grafton bowed his head. "You have a good eye, madam."

The compliment warmed her. "I love horses."

"Then you shall no doubt appreciate Ariel."

The groom walked a beautiful mare toward her. Ariel was well behaved but not in the least bit dull. The sparkle in the mare's eyes promised a fine ride.

"She is beautiful," Lucinda said as the groom assisted her into the sidesaddle.

"She is that. Much too pretty to pass over last year when I looked in at Tattersall's, and fine bloodlines besides. Her sire is one of Rothwell's steeds. My mother prefers the roan, so you may use Ariel as often as you wish."

"Thank you." She scratched between the mare's ears and fluffed her black forelock. Ariel was a dark bay with black socks, mane, and tail. Her face had a white mask in the shape of a teardrop.

"We can go slowly. 'Tis only five miles."

"Do not worry, sir. I assure you that I am up for a bit of stretch." Lucinda grinned, feeling exhilarated. The day was mild and the sun peeked out from behind huge puffy white clouds. Besides, she had never seen Lord Grafton more amiable. She urged Ariel forward into a trot and followed Lord Grafton upon Horatio out of the drive.

They arrived at Ivy Park after a leisurely ride. Grafton was impressed with Lucinda's prowess in the saddle. She rode well and treated his mare with gentle instruction. It amused him how often she cooed at the animal. Ariel responded by perking her ears forward every time Lucinda spoke to her.

"I think she likes you," Grafton said as they entered the Darrow stables.

Lucinda's cheeks were a rosy red from the exertion, her blue eyes clear and smiling. "The feeling is indeed mutual. Ariel is a sweet goer."

The groomsmen took their horses and Grafton offered Lucinda his arm. He noticed her hesitation and wondered at the cause. Was it him or the group that awaited them? "Are you not looking forward to tea?" He gave her an encouraging smile. Entering Ivy Park was hardly a comfortable place after yesterday.

She had lost the rosy glow to her cheeks and the sparkle in her eyes. "I shall make haste in signing and stay only as long as you deem necessary."

"It is not a lion's den we enter," he said.

"It may as well be," she whispered.

Lord Grafton patted her hand. "I shall be there to give you support."

She stopped walking, her expression thoughtful, as if she was not quite sure how to respond. She looked into his eyes and said softly, "Again, I am in your debt."

Grafton's heart thumped a little harder in his chest at the sincerity in her gaze. His offer of support had surprised them both. But she was not a troublesome female. In fact, he rather thought she was handling the entire tragedy with considerable pluck. "Come," he said, not wishing to stand outside gazing at her like a mooncalf.

The butler announced their arrival and Lady Darrow met them with open arms. "Come in, come in. Just in time. I have ordered tea."

Grafton noted that Lady Willow sat near the fire amid Sir Alaric's relatives and some of the local gentry. Mr. Lewes had remained as well. He stood near the fire, a deep scowl upon his face.

When Grafton sat down next to Lucinda, he noticed the titters and whispers between Sir Leonard's sisters. The two women were married, and their husbands, along with Sir Leonard and another man, played whist at a nearby table.

All were dressed in various degrees of mourning. There was enough black and gray clothing to depress anyone's spirits. But the lively atmosphere of a house party was at odds with the somber occasion. He could hardly expect every guest to exhibit long faces and gloominess, but such sentiments would have made him more comfortable.

He watched each guest carefully as tea was served. He wondered who among them was guilty of murdering Sir Alaric. He supposed if Robbie did not turn up any information about those present in this drawing room, he would have to review the guest list of Lucinda's wedding, which was a daunting thought.

Throughout tea, Lucinda spoke only when someone asked her a question directly. Sir Leonard's sisters chattered to themselves and Lady Darrow fluttered between Lucinda and the other women present like a goose with a scattered flock. She clearly was uncomfortable and Grafton wondered why. Most everyone ignored Mr. Lewes.

When they had finished their tea, Lucinda quietly asked, "Is Mr. Spenlow ready to see me?"

"I nearly forgot." Lady Darrow clapped her hands together, then stood. "He has been busy indeed, to not join us for tea. Come, Lucinda." Lady Darrow's eyes narrowed. "Let us go find him."

Grafton felt the hairs rise on his neck. He stood and noticed he was the only man who had done so. He felt a strong urge to accompany Lucinda—to protect her. He could hardly follow the ladies without looking like a fool.

Lady Darrow cast him a coy glance. "Do not worry, Grafton. She will not be gone long."

Grafton gritted his teeth. He did not know which irritated him more: Lady Darrow's informal use of his name or her veiled implication that he *was* a lovesick mooncalf. Either way, Lady Darrow was a mushroom. He sat down.

Lady Willow made her way toward him. "Would you care for more tea, my lord?" she asked, her voice soft and refined.

"Please."

She poured expertly and then sat down in the chair Lucinda had just vacated. "A terrible tragedy, losing Sir Alaric in such an accident. How fortunate that his young wife was left unhurt."

"Indeed." He sipped his tea.

"I heard that she endured nothing more than a few bruises."

Grafton narrowed his gaze.

Lady Willow smiled pleasantly. She had merely stated the obvious and that was all. Perhaps he was overreacting, but what else could he do? Sir Alaric Darrow was murdered and he'd bet a bull's-eye the killer stayed at Ivy Park. He took another sip. "Very fortunate," he said.

"But then her tender age, no doubt, helped her to recover so quickly."

"Indeed."

Lady Willow realized that he was not much of a conversationalist and quieted her questions. She poured more tea for herself and returned to her conversation with Sir Leonard's sisters.

Grafton relaxed. He need do nothing but wait until Lucinda returned.

Lucinda signed her name for the last time. She rubbed her hands upon the skirt of her habit, anxious to be gone. Conscious of her disquiet, Mr. Spenlow hurried through the process and offered her copies of what she had signed. She would go over everything with Lord Grafton when she rallied the courage to ask him.

She was anxious to quit Ivy Park. The houseguests did not want her there. They resented what she had been given by Alaric. Mr. Lewes did nothing but scowl at her through tea. Her nerves tense, she returned to the drawing room to say a quick farewell.

When they made their way to the stables, Lord Grafton asked, "Did the papers make sense?"

"Mr. Spenlow was very clear plus he gave me copies." She patted her deep pockets. "He suggested I wait before signing over those shares as well."

"A wise man." Grafton nodded.

" 'At least until the *business* surrounding Alaric's death is resolved' were his exact words."

"I could have my solicitor review the documents with you if you have any concerns," he said.

"Thank you." She felt a prick of disappointment. She would rather go over the papers with Lord Grafton alone, but she certainly did not wish to presume upon his recent good nature. With a start, Lucinda realized that with the exception of her mother, Lord Grafton had become the only person she trusted.

When they reached the barn, their mounts were ready and Lord Grafton assisted her into the saddle. "So how do you feel?" he asked. "Any pains?"

"Not now, but I shall no doubt eat my words later when stiffness sets in. Regardless of the accident, it has been a while since last I rode."

Lord Grafton looked concerned. "Perhaps we should go slow."

"If you please, I would rather give Ariel her head and see how she does at a gallop."

"Are you quite certain?" He looked uncertain of her ability.

Lucinda grinned. "I am."

"Very well, we will take that worn path back to Arden Hall." He pointed. " 'Tis a bit longer, but good for hard riding."

They left the yard of Ivy Park and headed west through the woods. In moments the path widened and Lord Grafton gestured for her to take the lead and set the pace.

Lucinda did not hesitate a moment. She urged Ariel forward much to Horatio's dissatisfaction. Lord Grafton held the stallion back with complete control, but his mount was not happy to give over the lead.

Lucinda laughed and eased Ariel into a smooth canter. "There you go, my sweet," she whispered. "Let us see what you are made of."

She slackened the reins and let the horse choose the gait. Ariel was quick to respond. With a dip of her head, the mare took off into a full gallop.

They moved as one, horse and rider, and Lucinda felt more alive than she had in months. Thoughts of

Alaric's terrible death, her inheritance, and even Lord Grafton were pushed aside. She wanted only to focus on the sheer exhilaration of a late autumn ride.

Decaying leaves crunched beneath Ariel's hooves and the cool air smelled deliciously sweet. They came to a clearing and Lucinda glanced back at Lord Grafton. He looked relaxed and was nearly smiling. He enjoyed the ride as much as she. He held his stallion in check, which allowed her and Ariel to move with the wind ahead of them.

And then something went terribly wrong.

Her seat was no longer solid and Ariel stumbled out of gait. Lucinda was pulled under and she fell. She landed on the ground with a hard thud that left her reeling.

She felt the ground shake and heard the thundering of hooves. She had the sense to roll away from Horatio before she was trampled. And then everything went dark.

"Lady Darrow!"

Lucinda heard Lord Grafton's distraught voice through a painful fog. She opened her eyes to find his worried gaze peering back.

"Are you hurt?"

It felt as if the ground beneath her was spinning. She could not form the words to speak.

"Good God!" Lord Grafton felt along her neck and shoulders. "Where are you hurt?" He continued down each arm to her ribs, his voice loud and terse. "Where do you hurt?"

"My head," she finally groaned. She wore a cap of painful throbbing and closed her eyes against the glaring sunshine.

"Look at me. No, no. Do not close your eyes! Look at me."

She tried to comply and failed. It felt much better to keep her eyes closed.

"Lucinda!" he said quickly.

That got her attention. She had not given him leave to address her thus but she rather liked the sound of her name on his lips.

"Can you see me?"

"Of course I can see you."

Relief washed over his face and he sat back on his haunches. "What happened?"

"I do not know." She tried to sit up, which made matters worse. She flopped back down and closed her eyes.

"Do not sleep." He roused her with a shake.

"I cannot keep my eyes open. The light hurts too much."

"Just sit still. You've no doubt suffered a concussion. Even so, stay awake." He stood.

She squinted and watched Lord Grafton run away from her. It hurt far too much to raise her head enough to see where. She lay with her head reeling and her stomach roiling. Shielding her eyes with her hand, she wondered how she had come to this pass. One moment she had been moving faster than a flash of lightning and then she was on the ground.

"Here." He placed a cold wet cloth upon her head. "Keep this on."

"Where did you go?"

"There is a stream just beyond those trees."

"Where is Ariel? Is she all right?"

He watched her closely. "She is fine."

"What happened?"

"You fell off."

She shifted and winced. "I have not fallen off a horse in years."

His worry-filled gray eyes peered into hers. "The entire saddle came off. The girth must not have been tightened."

She turned her head and saw a heap of leather not very far off. Lord Grafton followed her gaze, then walked over and picked up the saddle. He examined it closely and swore. She never expected the high-and-mighty Lord Grafton to use such language.

"What is it?" she called out, which caused her ears to ring harder.

He brought the saddle near. "The girth was ripped. You could have been killed."

She felt dizzy again.

"The leather strap has been cut. See here where the connected part tore away?"

"How?"

Lord Grafton hesitated, as if searching for the right words. "To be quite frank, I think someone at Ivy Park tampered with your saddle."

The grim reality of his words caused her to shiver. She closed her eyes and remembered the vision of Alaric twisted and gasping. And now this. She did not wish to die.

Lord Grafton knelt down next to her. His voice low, he asked, "Can you sit up? We need to get you home." He took off his jacket and draped it about her shoulders.

She realized the wet cloth was his cravat when she saw the strong column of his bare neck. She handed the bit of linen back to him.

He shook it out with a snap. "I'll get the horses." Then he touched her shoulder. "Stay here."

She nodded and that small movement caused her to see stars.

He returned with Ariel's reins tied to Horatio's saddle. "I am going to lift you. Tell me if I hurt you." He bent down and picked her up with fluid grace as if she weighed little. He hoisted her into the saddle, then swung up behind her. "Ready?"

"Yes." But she felt terribly unsteady.

He pulled her close and whispered, "Lean into me."

She did as he bid. The warmth of his chest was welcome. He held her firm with one arm. His hand splayed across her waist and heat radiated through her. She could no longer hold her head up, so she rested against Lord Grafton's broad shoulder.

"And so we repeat history," he murmured, recalling how they had done this before.

"I am so sorry," she whispered. She had been nothing but trouble for him.

"Do not be," he said close to her ear. His lips brushed her temple. "Hang on tight and stay awake."

But she squeezed her eyes shut in an attempt to ward off the fear that ate away at her insides. She could hardly sleep. Someone wanted her dead.

Grafton kept Horatio moving at a sedate walk. His horse stepped carefully as if he knew the delicate condition of the additional rider. Grafton nearly chuckled at his sensitive horse, but Lucinda's head injury was no laughing matter.

Sir Alaric's words proved to have merit. He had worried for his young wife's safety and Grafton had discarded those concerns as mere paranoia. Obviously, Grafton had been wrong. His promise to protect Lucinda took on new meaning. He could not let her out of his sight or away from Arden Hall until he had those responsible for this attack in his clutches.

Anger did not mix well with disgust and Grafton felt both in good measure. Sir Leonard's wife had known they were coming. She no doubt announced as much to her guests. Any one of them could have made arrangements for Lucinda's saddle to be cut.

He must inform Robbie immediately. They needed to send someone back to Ivy Park to find out who had tampered with the saddle.

"Please do not tell my mother what happened. Not about the cut girth strap," Lucinda said.

"Does she know about Sir Alaric's poisoning?"

"No."

He did not think it wise to keep such a thing from a parent. But then he had kept his own mother in the dark all this time. That would change. With this new threat, Grafton needed his mother's help. "Perhaps she should know you are in danger."

"No." She was adamant. "She will only worry herself into sickness. Besides, we will go home soon enough."

"Out of the question."

"But—"

His tone softened. "You cannot leave. If your mother must return to your siblings, I will send her in my carriage with men for protection. But I can hardly keep you safe if you are miles away. Besides," he said, "you cannot travel in this condition."

She silently absorbed his orders. "It will only cause more gossip if I stay."

He did not care to be the subject of lurid whispers that he had designs upon Sir Alaric's widow, but what choice did he have? He had given his word of honor that he would protect her. In order to do so, he had to keep her close. "I do not care," he said.

"You are a poor liar, my lord," Lucinda said.

He snorted his contempt. Was he so transparent?

"Forgive me for placing you in this position." Her voice was low, hoarse.

His frustration rose. "For pity's sake, you had no hand in it." He did not like the position he now found himself in any more than she did, but he had made a promise.

Lucinda's presence at Arden Hall well after the funeral would raise eyebrows and even London might hear of it, but there was nothing to be done. He must watch over her. He let out of sigh of resignation.

"I am glad that you finally believe I had no hand in Alaric's death," she said with an insulted air of dignity.

She hardly would have killed herself in an attempt to prove her innocence. "I beg your pardon for answering sharp," he said.

"You are forgiven, my lord."

"You needn't 'my lord' me forever and a day. Call me Grafton."

"Very well. And you must call me Lucinda."

"I believe I already have."

He needed a plausible excuse to explain Lucinda's presence at Arden Hall and keep his reputation in tact. But what reason could there be?

Chapter Seven

*O*nce again, Grafton entered his home with Lucinda in his arms. Only this time, her condition worried him something fierce. Her head lolled from side to side and she could barely keep her eyes open. "Stay awake, Lucinda," he whispered.

Her eyes fluttered open and she gazed at him with a furrowed brow as if trying to figure out who he was.

"Naughton!" he bellowed.

Grafton had crossed the marble floor and taken the first few steps up the stairs when his butler hurried down the hall to see what was the matter. "Fetch Mrs. Bronwell and my mother, will you?"

His butler looked more than a little worried. "Is she all right, sir?"

"She will be. Now go quickly. And send for the doctor also."

Naughton did as he was bid, but only after a few moments' mindful hesitation. His butler did not show concern often, but obviously his sentiments for

Lucinda were real. Grafton shook his head. Lucinda had been here less than a week and his entire household was enamored of her.

He carried her to her room and managed to open the door without dropping her. Once inside, he strode to the bed, pulled back the coverlet, and lowered her gently.

She stirred. "Where—"

"Home." He unlaced her boots.

She sat up straighter, her eyes wide as she watched him pull first one boot off and drop it to the floor, and then the other. "Thank you." Her eyelids drooped.

He tucked her feet under the covers. "You mustn't sleep yet, not until after the doctor arrives."

"But I am so tired." She dropped her head forward and rubbed the back of her neck.

When she looked up at him, a stray curl fell in front of her eyes.

Without thinking, he brushed back the lock of golden hair, and the curl wound around his thumb. He stared at it, then at her, and she did not look away from him. She was perhaps the most beautiful woman he had ever seen.

"Goodness, what happened?" Mrs. Bronwell bustled into the room followed by his mother.

He let go of the golden curl. He turned to see the worried faces of his mother and Mrs. Bronwell, both waiting for an answer. "She took a tumble off of Ariel."

"I never liked that mare," his mother said.

"No broken bones, but she hit her head quite hard.

I have sent for the physician to be sure, but I think she may have a concussion. We need to see to it that she remains awake."

His mother gave Mrs. Bronwell an encouraging hug. "She will be just fine. Lucinda is strong and healthy. Are you not, dear?"

Lucinda gave a muffled agreement and then yawned.

Mrs. Bronwell paid no attention. She looked straight through Grafton. "Lucinda does not fall off horses, my lord. She is an accomplished rider. My husband kept a substantial stable until he died."

Grafton was not about to lie to her. He'd leave that up to Lucinda. "I am certain your daughter will explain exactly what happened when she is up to it. One moment we were moving along and then she was on the ground. Perhaps her balance is not quite restored from the carriage accident."

"Of course, you are right," Mrs. Bronwell said, looking remorseful for challenging him. She hurried to her daughter's side.

Poor Mrs. Bronwell. She must know something was afoot. Deep lines of worry etched her brow. He did not recall them being that pronounced when she had first arrived. "I will have our housekeeper bring tea," he said, heading for the door. "If you need anything, please let me know."

"You have been all that is kind," Mrs. Bronwell said.

"Come along, Mother," Grafton said.

"Grafton," Lucinda called out.

He turned. "Yes?"

She hesitated. "Perhaps some biscuits with the tea."

He smiled. "I will see to it." Once the door was closed and he and his mother were safely down the hall, he said, "We need to talk."

"Very well, perhaps—"

"Can we go to your rooms?"

His mother looked worried. "Of course, dear."

Inside his mother's vast apartment, he ordered tea and biscuits for Lucinda. Then he paced the floor.

"You will tread a hole in that carpet. Now spill it. What is going on?"

He looked at his mother, seated comfortably in an overstuffed chair. He hated to be the one to increase the alarm he read in her eyes, but he needed her help. "Lucinda's fall was no accident."

His mother's eyes grew wider and more fearful. "What do you mean?"

"The girth was cut."

"What!"

"Someone wanted her to fall. Someone at Ivy Park."

"She could have been killed. Who would do such a thing?"

He took a deep breath. "The same person who poisoned Sir Alaric."

"Poison? I thought—"

"Mother, the carriage accident was nothing more than an attempt to cover up the real reason for Sir Alaric's death. His brandy was laced with arsenic and I will find the person responsible."

"Goodness, Dougie. Have you gone to the constable?"

"Not yet. With the inheritance the way it is, the constable might consider Lucinda the likely culprit and lock her up, and that would be the end of it. I could not allow that to happen. You can see, now, why I must keep her here at Arden Hall. I gave Sir Alaric my word that I'd see to her safety."

His mother looked appalled. "Why did you not tell me this earlier?"

"I did not wish to distress you unduly."

"I am no feeble woman!" His mother abruptly stood. With her head held high, she went to a small sideboard, and reached for a decanter of sherry and poured a small amount in a glass. "Would you care for some?"

He shook his head. "No, thank you. Originally, I thought that perhaps Lucinda might have had a hand in what happened. But I see now that is impossible."

"Lucinda?" His mother looked at him as if he had grown a second head. "Dougie, she is a dear girl. How could you possibly think she is capable of such a terrible deed?"

"If you would have seen her in Town . . ."

"Oh, for heaven's sake. Yes, yes, she is a fortune hunter—and from what I have surmised, a very bad one if she only managed to wrestle a proposal from someone like Sir Alaric Darrow. With her looks, she should have done much better." His mother sipped her sherry. "She should have nabbed someone like you."

"Me?"

"You went to London to find a bride. Why not her?"

He ran a hand through his hair. "You cannot be serious." But she was. She looked at him expectantly, waiting for him to explain what was wrong with Lucinda. For a moment, he could think of nothing to say.

He recalled how she had looked this evening when he laid her upon her bed. Her sleepy blue eyes and waves of golden hair . . . He caught himself in time. "She is hardly respectable."

His mother raised her chin with a sniff. "I do not believe that. Her manners are very nice. The servants adore her. She is far more worthy of respect than many. She is completely unspoiled."

That was indeed true, but he did not care to let what he had witnessed in Town go. "I know what I saw with my own eyes. Her gowns were cut down to there." He pointed to the middle of his chest.

"A desperate woman will do things out of the ordinary if she must to protect or provide for her family."

"Would she resort to murder?"

"For shame!" His mother looked furious. "You know as well as I do that Lucinda could not have poisoned her husband."

He held up his hand. "Yes, I know. At least, I know that now. Besides, she would hardly cut her own saddle, then gallop to her doom just to throw off my suspicions."

Her mother's face went pale. "Dougie, she could have been killed."

"Yes." He took a deep, shuddering breath. He had watched it unfold before his very eyes and he had been powerless to keep her from hitting the ground. Had she not rolled out of the way . . .

He stalked to his mother's sherry decanter and poured himself a glass. After taking a deep swallow, he set the goblet on the tray and faced his mother.

Her eyes narrowed. "What are you going to do?"

"I have Robbie working on gathering information about the guests at Ivy Park."

"You think it is one of Sir Alaric's relatives, then?"

"Frankly, Mother, I do not know. But I cannot find out if they are there and we are here."

"Perhaps we should invite them here to Arden Hall."

He scratched his chin. "On what pretense?"

His mother grinned and he realized he should have made her wise to the whole situation sooner. "What would you say to a holiday house party? That would give you enough time to ferret out the killer."

"Invite them all here? Mother, are you sure?"

"Yes. 'Tis not quite the way I would wish to spend my Christmastide, but I do not know how else you can gather them together under one roof."

He liked it. In fact, it was genius. "Arden Hall will be a controlled environment."

"And we will make sure Lucinda is kept safe and sound the whole time. The servants can help."

He looked up. "Do not tell the servants. The fewer people who know about what we are up to, the better." He did not like the idea of inviting a murderer anywhere near Lucinda, but what choice did he have? Until the culprit had been brought to justice, her life would always be in danger.

"So we should prepare to entertain a possible murderer for the holidays." His mother gave him a cheeky grin.

Her dark humor was not lost on him. He chuckled in response. "Indeed. It makes for an interesting party." He rose to leave and turned serious. "Thank you, Mother. I appreciate your willingness to help."

She smiled. "Of course, my son."

"A holiday party?" Lucinda asked two days later when she joined Lord Grafton for breakfast. Each of their mothers remained in their rooms with a tray, so she and Lord Grafton were completely alone.

"Yes," he said. "With everyone under my roof, I will have a much better chance to catch the killer."

"But Christmas is three weeks away."

"All the more time to gather information about our guests."

She wiped her mouth with her napkin and pushed her nearly empty plate away. "Lord Grafton, I appreciate your kindness, but I wish to go home. I cannot be away from my family for so long, especially at Christmas."

"You cannot leave yet."

She cocked her head. "My mother must return to Bronley Manor and I have every intention of going with her."

"Lucinda, it is not safe." He concentrated on buttering another piece of toast. "Have you told your mother that your saddle had been cut?"

"No."

"Shall I?"

"You wouldn't." But she knew that he would.

"Yes, I would." His voice softened. "I know you want to go home. I do not blame you one whit, but think about what happened yesterday. Do you truly think the monster that sliced your saddle will allow distance to interfere with his nefarious plans? Whoever is responsible for Sir Alaric's death is now looking for your own. You will be safest here."

With a sinking feeling, she knew she had lost the battle. "What if the saddle was cut here?" she asked in a small voice.

"Impossible. The gash was three-fourths of the way through the leather. Had it been done here, you would have fallen on your way to Ivy Park, not on the return trip."

His argument made perfect sense. Her home would no longer be safe, if someone truly wanted her dead. And not for the world would she invite that kind of trouble to Bronley Manor. She felt his warm hand cover her own and took comfort from it.

"I am sorry." He gave her hand a squeeze.

She turned her hand to grip his and whispered, "I did not want this."

"Why Sir Alaric?" Lord Grafton asked.

"He chose me."

"Were there no others?"

She sighed. "Yes, but my aunt was very protective, if you can believe that. I can only assume that the gentlemen who asked permission to pay their addresses were apprised of how dire my family situation had become and they changed their minds. I had to start over and over." She remembered the disappointment, the shame of failing. It was terribly demeaning.

"Perhaps if you would have displayed more decorum and less—" He stopped, his face aflame.

"What, my lord? Less décolletage?" She had

shocked him. His eyes were wide with censure, but not the stark disapproval she had seen before.

His gaze softened. "Yes."

"My first Season, I was everything that was proper and nice." She looked into his eyes. "You were not in London the spring of 'nineteen, were you?"

"No. My father had died the previous summer."

"My sympathies."

He waved it away, then returned to holding her hand. "No matter, go on."

Bitterness crept into her tone. "Midway through my first Season, I fell into a pond at the Collingtons' breakfast. The day had been warm, so I chose to forgo a chemise. My gown was not so thin—who would know? Well, after a thorough dousing, everyone knew. After that, I did not lack for gentlemen callers. But even though several were warm in funds, many offered carte blanche rather than wedding bells and righting family debts." She took a sip of tea. "What does a poor girl have to offer besides a pretty face and form?"

"And so you decided to display your delectable form for one and all?" Again the censure, but his eyes had darkened to the color of molten steel.

She did not think he had noticed her form. "I could no longer afford my own sensibilities, and neither could my family. A larger net catches more fish!"

"Even rotten ones?" He threaded his fingers through hers.

"I had run out of time. My family's hopes had been pinned upon me—I needed to wed after my first Season and here I was returning for a second. I had to marry a wealthy man or all would be lost."

"Was it worth it?" he asked quietly, his thumb tracing a distracting path along the back of her hand.

"What if Arden Hall and your father's legacy were at risk? Would you not do everything in your power to save them, even marry for wealth?"

His gaze was steady and his dark gray eyes reflected empathy. "I never quite looked at it that way before. Your father, was he a good man?"

Lucinda smiled. "The very best of men, but he waged an uphill battle with debt his entire life. Bronley Manor was sadly entailed when he inherited it and the few investments he placed did not turn around as he had hoped. Then he died from a sudden seizure."

"My father was not a good man and I have done everything in my power to keep his legacy of vice away from me and mine. But even so, I better understand your situation."

She let her gaze drop. Lord Grafton still held her hand and she liked the feel of his warm strength far too much. She pulled away immediately. "I beg your pardon."

His face registered surprise as though he had not intended to touch her so. "Sometimes a firm hand helps when you discuss something painful."

"Indeed," she said. She had not thought him capable of compassion before. She was pleased that he had proved her wrong. Underneath his arrogant exterior, Lord Grafton was a kindhearted man, and she felt drawn to him. "If we may turn back to the holiday party."

"Yes?"

"If I must remain here over Christmastide and you

plan for a house filled with guests, might I add a few more to your numbers?"

Grafton kept his hands firmly in front of him. What had possessed him to hold her so? But her eyes were so blue and her face so incredibly sweet, Grafton knew he would deny her nothing. "And the added few?"

"My family. I have never been away from them over the holiday. If I cannot go home to them due to the circumstances, can we not bring them here to me?"

Just how large was this family for whom she felt compelled to sacrifice her happiness? "Do you think it wise? I cannot guarantee their safety."

"There are no guarantees in life, my lord. My mother will watch over them and they in turn will keep me safe."

Grafton scratched his chin. "How many are there?"

"My mother, whom you have met, my two sisters, both of whom are complete dears and very capable, and my little brother, Thomas. He will be quite in awe of you, sir."

Grafton chuckled. "Will *he*? How so?"

"Thomas has been in alt over his studies of the knights of the Round Table. He will no doubt wish to cast you as one of them. His favorite, of course, is Sir Gawain—the virtuous fellow who fought the Green Knight."

Did she find him virtuous then? He wished he knew. In fact, he wondered what the fair Lucinda thought of him. "How old is your brother?"

"Ten. He is good boy." She took another sip of tea. "Cold."

"Would you care for new?"

"No, no, 'tis my punishment for chatting instead of drinking."

He smiled. "Indeed." He had rather enjoyed their coze this morning. The house had been oddly quiet as she recuperated from her fall. He had missed seeing her in the breakfast room. "Let me take the matter up with my mother. Perhaps we might enlist reinforcements to guard the children."

Lucinda nodded. "Do you really think we might catch the person responsible for killing Alaric at this party?" She tried to sound unconcerned and matter-of-fact, but he heard the tremor in her voice.

"I hope so."

"How will we know?"

"My solicitor is looking into the past history of each person named in Sir Alaric's will. Hopefully something in one of the guests' past will provide us with a clue."

"Even mine?"

Grafton paused. They were getting on so well, he did not wish to put them at odds. "Regrettably yes, even yours."

She gazed at him. "Do you trust no one?"

"Very few. In my life's experience, trust is a costly gift I can rarely bestow."

"As I have said before, Lord Grafton, I have nothing to hide."

He felt sure that was true, but he had given Robbie his orders before he truly knew her. "And as I have said before, you may call me Grafton."

She looked disappointed, almost hurt. "If you will excuse me, *Grafton*. There is much to be done to prepare for your party. I must explain to my mother the reasons for not returning home with her and perhaps I might offer your mother my help in planning for your guests." She stood.

He did as well. "She would greatly appreciate your assistance. And so would I."

" 'Tis the least I can do."

Grafton sat back down after she had left. He poured himself another cup of coffee with the intention of finishing his newspaper, but he could not concentrate. He had held Lucinda's hand through their entire conversation. And she had not pulled her hand away until she realized how long they had twined their fingers with near abandon.

One thing he had to admit about Lucinda Bronwell—she had considerable composure. But every now and then he glimpsed a crack. He should not be surprised at offering her comfort at such times. The fact that she hardly showed her fear was all the more to her credit.

She had given over her argument to return home quickly, which proved that she looked to him to protect her—counted on him to do so. She could have been killed the other day and he was not about to let another incident like that happen.

Chapter Eight

The morning of Christmas Eve, Grafton sat at his desk reading a note from Robbie, delivered by way of a cheeky stable boy. His solicitor had taken a room at the Rose and Slipper the previous day in order to tie up some loose ends. Robbie assured him that he would arrive at Arden Hall in time for the annual Grafton open house and bring him up-to-date on the investigation.

His letter further explained that the man he had hired to look into the Darrows' backgrounds had completed much of his information gathering, but was given leave to spend the holiday with his family near Oxford.

This same man had had no luck in finding any information at Ivy Park regarding Lucinda's cut saddle girth nearly three weeks ago. Whoever had done the deed did so with utmost stealth, much to Grafton's irritation. He crumpled the letter and threw it into the grate, watching the flames engulf the paper.

Robbie's investigations had turned up nothing

about the Bronwells contrary to what Lucinda had told him. Their financial situation had been even bleaker than she had painted it. The rest of Sir Alaric's beneficiaries were also having difficulties with their funds, with the exception of Lady Willow.

Sir Alaric's nephew was so deep in debt 'twas small wonder the man remained in a brandy-induced haze. Mr. Lewes, Sir Alaric's business partner, had the most to gain if something happened to Lucinda. His business dealings had taken a turn for disaster due to a shipwreck and a poor investment placed on the 'Change. He needed those shares in order to borrow the funds necessary to recoup his recent losses.

Grafton let out a sigh. Tomorrow night was the start of his house party to catch Sir Alaric's murderer. He wanted the thing done and over so his life might return to normal. Perhaps, once Lucinda went home with her family, he might revert to his usual self.

For the past three weeks he had done his best to avoid Lucinda. It was not terribly difficult since his mother had kept her busy planning the holiday party. But after Lucinda recovered from her concussion, she had been ready to ride Ariel. He trusted no one else to accompany her, so he rode with her. At least on horseback, one could refrain from any depth of conversation. But he watched her every movement and enjoyed the grace she displayed.

He did not like the way his heart skipped a beat when he suddenly saw her, nor how his hands fairly itched to hold hers. His attraction to Lucinda Bronwell grew with every day she spent under his roof and he wanted no more of it. She was a recent widow. He knew better than to yearn for something he should not even contemplate until after a year of mourning had passed.

Her family had arrived and they would no doubt take up much of her time. He had not the heart to refuse Lucinda's request that he invite them to Arden Hall for Christmastide. And his mother had assured him that the two youngest children would be well protected by her artist friend, Lady Anne Telford.

With everything in order, Grafton decided he should keep his wits about him, which meant keeping his distance from Lucinda. At least there were four Bronwells to act as a buffer between them, keeping them both safe.

Lucinda woke late. It was Christmas Eve and there was much to do. The first order of business was to attend church services. Her family had arrived yesterday and the reunion was both joyous and loud. She had missed them terribly. Poor Lord Grafton, his home had been overrun with Bronwells! After the introductions, he took refuge in his study until dinner.

Her sisters looked well and behaved nicely considering this was their first trip anywhere. Bethany, who had just turned seventeen, was in alt to be included in a grown-up party. Margaret, only thirteen, was relegated to the nursery with their ten-year-old brother, Thomas, down from Eton for the holiday. A friend of Lady Grafton's would act as governess and protector until the party ended on Twelfth Night.

Dinner had been a pleasant and festive affair even if the girls tended to stare and Thomas beleaguered their host over the subject of traipsing about Grafton land for the Yule log. Lucinda's heart had warmed considerably when Lord Grafton joined them after dinner in the drawing room and entertained them all with stories of Christmas pixies that hid in Yule logs in order to wreak havoc within the home the coming year.

Lucinda had remained busy the past three weeks helping Lady Grafton with preparations for Christmastide. No more accidents or threats to her life had occurred since the ride to Ivy Park, but Lord Grafton kept her on a short tether and very close to Arden Hall.

He escorted her to church services on Sundays and restricted her walks through his courtyard, and the rare occasions in his company were spent riding Grafton land.

Time had flown by as she helped Lady Grafton with her plans to decorate the estate before it was opened to Lord Grafton's tenants, the local parishioners, and gentry from the nearby village of Arden. Lucinda also helped fashion baskets of baked goods and foodstuff for each family to take home from the customary Christmas Eve feast at Arden Hall.

She had been impressed by the amount in each basket, which had been ordered by Lord Grafton himself to be packed full. He was a generous man once a person got past his arrogance. Still, she was not yet entirely comfortable in his presence, but then he was too handsome by half.

Although she craved his attention, she was determined not to seek it. He still thought of her with apprehension, no doubt, because of her behavior in London. She vowed to do nothing disrespectful or inappropriate. She was a newly made widow, after all, and bound by convention to observe full mourning for at least another eleven months.

But the holidays allowed the rules of mourning to be bent, and tomorrow, the house party would commence. The invitations had long gone out to all who had been present at the reading of Alaric's will and all had accepted, no doubt due to curiosity if no other reason.

Lady Grafton had told her the holiday traditions of Arden Hall had never before been so grand. Having few living relatives, they usually entertained only a small group of friends.

Lucinda sat upon her bed, rubbing her eyes. She looked forward to the festivities regardless of the somber reason the guests had been invited.

A knock at the door got her out of bed, but before she could speak, her sisters bounced into the room. "Lucinda, you are only just rising?" Bethany held up a gown of rich yellow. "Do you think this fine enough for church?"

Lucinda yawned. They had stayed up far too late the previous evening. "Perhaps something warmer, dearest."

Bethany made a face. "What will you wear?"

Lucinda sighed. "Something new but black. Lady Grafton sent for the dressmaker from the village to take my measurements. I needed a few more mourning dresses for the party, so I shall probably wear one of my new gowns."

"Too bad that you must dress in blacks on Christmas Eve." Bethany sat upon the bed.

Lucinda smiled. "I do not mind." She did not care

what she wore as long as it was modest and she did not offend their host. "Besides," she added, "after all Sir Alaric has done for us, I am content to honor his memory."

Margaret asked, "Do you miss him?"

Lucinda was terribly sorry for his death, but she could hardly deny the sense of relief she felt. "I miss his kindness." It was true, and a safe way to respond.

Both sisters nodded, their exuberance subdued for only a moment. "Perhaps you might marry Lord Grafton," Margaret said. "He is very handsome."

Lucinda felt her face flame. "Margaret, do not say such a thing."

"Why not?"

"Because, goose"—Bethany pinched their little sister—"Lucy has to wait until her mourning period is over before she can remarry."

"Why?" Margaret did not understand the ways of society. Lucinda hoped that neither of her sisters ever encountered the difficulties she had faced.

"Because that is the way it is," Bethany said. "Although he is truly very handsome."

"Go on, both of you, and get dressed. We do not wish to be late." Her sisters left with giggles and Lucinda sighed.

Of course Lord Grafton was handsome. She tried to ignore the breadth of his shoulders and the darkness of his hair, which waved perfectly away from his strong, angular face. His gray eyes made her heart pound every time she looked into them. She sighed before she pulled the bell for the maid assigned to her. Lord Grafton wanted nothing more than to keep her safe until Alaric's killer could be found. To dream of anything more was courting heartache.

After she had washed and dressed, she met everyone in the large drawing room. Her gaze immediately sought out Lord Grafton. She simply could not help it. He and her brother, Thomas, stood together surveying the hearth.

"We can get a big log in there," her brother said.

"After luncheon, we shall venture out for our Yule log and greenery." He looked up and caught her staring, but did not look away.

Lucinda's heart flipped over.

"Are we ready to depart for services?" Lady Grafton had a merry twinkle in her eyes.

Lucinda felt caught. She knew her cheeks were bright red. Embarrassed, she looked down at her hands and pushed them into her muff. "Yes, of course."

They squeezed into two open carriages to make the short journey to Grafton Chapel. Once inside, they took their places in the Grafton family pews. Lucinda took care in choosing her seat. As usual, she did not dare sit next to Lord Grafton. It would only serve to fuel the gossipmongers, who clearly wondered why she remained at Arden Hall after Alaric's funeral. If she had heard the whispers, then Lord Grafton must have as well. She sat in the pew behind him with her mother and sisters, leaving Thomas to sit next to Lord Grafton.

"A pretty chapel," Bethany whispered in her ear.

"Newly renovated too," Lucinda said. She looked up into the rafters, which were painted pristine white. The wooden pews had been polished to a mellow shine. She wondered what the chapel had looked like before Lord Grafton had come into the title. He had told her the chapel was his first project as earl since his father had sorely neglected it for years.

An elderly curate with a friendly smile delivered a sermon of hope amid the greenery that was festooned with bright red ribbon. At the close of service, the curate and his wife handed each attendee a small tin of baked goods.

"Mrs. Grant's spice cakes are the very best," Lord Grafton said loudly enough for the lady to hear. "Something I look forward to each and every Christmas." His chest swelled with pride and he offered Lucinda his arm.

Mrs. Grant's cheeks grew pink and she waved his compliment away. "Go on with you, Grafton. They are merely simple goodies."

"Made better by your hand, Mrs. Grant." Lord Grafton bowed.

"They are a dear couple," Lucinda said as they stepped out into a misty gray morning.

No one appeared to be in a hurry to leave. Both tenants and villagers alike hung about wishing each other a happy Christmas even though the air was damp and chilly. But it was not nearly cold enough for Lucinda to shake the warm feeling that always enveloped her when Lord Grafton stood near.

She let her gaze travel the tall length of him. She laughed when he guarded his tin like a starving schoolboy. Lord Grafton's tin had more of the little cakes than most and he was not about to share them with anyone. He ate one, then reached for another. "Do not eat them all at once," she teased.

"But of course, I must. I will have my tin gone by luncheon. Wait until your brother takes a bite. He will be as smitten as I."

Lucinda laughed. "I appreciate you taking an interest in him. With only sisters to turn to, he has been a little lost since Father died."

His expression turned serious. "Thomas is a fine young man."

And so are you. Lucinda watched as Lord Grafton's attention was captured by one of his tenants. He reminded the man and his family that tonight they dined at Arden Hall. The man looked at Lord Grafton with respect. In fact, all the people she encountered looked at Lord Grafton the same way. She craved to be so esteemed.

Lord Grafton donned his sturdiest boots and warmest coat and waited for the others to join him by the main entrance. Luncheon had been rushed because the Bronwells were excited to gather greens. Lucinda's sisters promised the same beauty as their older sister, and their blond-headed brother possessed strength of character rare in one so young. They were a warm, nice family. His mother had taken to them quickly and so had he.

Since her family's arrival, Lucinda gathered her siblings around her like a hen with her chicks. Although Mrs. Bronwell was their mother, it was obvious that Lucinda held a position of authority. She kept control of matters in her own calm way, alleviating her mother's responsibilities as much as possible.

He could see why Lucinda had taken on the task of saving the family fortune. Seeing how much she loved her family, he understood her actions in marrying for money.

He suspected the hardship of their loss and grief had served to strengthen their family bond rather than weaken it. He found their love and appreciation of one another refreshing, something he hoped to cultivate in his own family, when he started one.

He remembered Lucinda during the Season, desperately searching for a wealthy man to wed to protect her tender sisters from having to do the same. Her sacrifice was honorable. He had known so little about her then.

His mother's words echoed through his thoughts. *"She should have nabbed someone like you."*

He heard footsteps down the hall and looked up to see young Thomas walking toward him.

"The girls will be down directly," Thomas informed him.

"Very well. Master Thomas, should we check on our wagon?"

"Indeed, sir." The boy grinned.

They exited the door into sunshine that chased away the damp. It was a perfect day to hunt for Christmas greenery and, of course, a Yule log. After Grafton checked with his groom, the large wagon was harnessed to a workhorse in preparation to make way to the woods.

Thomas scratched the horse's nose. "A fine sturdy horse, my lord. After Lucy got engaged, we were able to purchase one for our fields." He puffed up his chest. "I named him Buttons."

"Buttons?" Grafton followed the lad's lead. "Why such a name?"

"He had a habit of chewing my buttons!" The boy smiled, glad that Grafton had asked.

Grafton ruffled Thomas' hair. "A fine name indeed. Come, we best meet your sisters at the steps. There is much to be done." He walked the horse and wagon to the front of the house.

The door opened and three Bronwell ladies stepped outside. They were dressed warmly and beaming with smiles.

"But where is Mrs. Bronwell?" Grafton asked.

"Helping your mother with preparations for this evening's open house," Lucinda answered.

"Very well, then, ladies." He bowed. "Your chariot."

This caused the Bronwell girls to giggle. Despite her black wool habit, Lucinda looked young and carefree, a sprig of holly pinned onto her collar. Her cheeks were rosy and her blue eyes sparkled. He had never seen her look more lovely.

"Hurry up, girls," young Thomas said in a most demanding voice. "We haven't all day. There is much to do."

"We shall be there soon enough, Thomas," Lucinda scolded.

Grafton stifled a smile at the lad's use of his own words. He assisted each young lady into the wagon, loaded with cutting shears and baskets. Blankets had also been placed in the wagon, but since the air was mild, the girls sat upon them instead of covering themselves.

Grafton checked that each lady was comfortably seated; then, with a click of the reins, he announced, "We are off." Thomas sat upon the bench in front with him.

They traveled deep into the woods between Ivy Park and Arden Hall in search of a felled log that satisfied young Thomas' measurements. With that completed, they marked the log with a ribbon so they could fetch it later. They traveled the edge of the woods and into the fields to gather holly, strands of ivy, and boughs of evergreen. The fragrance of the clippings filled Grafton with the spirit of Christmas and good cheer. The Bronwells made this simple holiday task enjoyable, one he would fondly remember.

"No mistletoe, Lord Grafton?" Bethany asked.

"Not on my list." Grafton peeked at Lucinda who avoided his gaze. He watched as she licked her lips and wondered what it would be like to kiss her luscious mouth. He changed the direction of his thoughts and answered Miss Bethany more politely. "It does not grow here and I never thought to purchase some in the village."

"Too bad," Bethany said with a pointed glance at her older sister.

Too bad, indeed. Grafton smiled. Miss Bethany rivaled his mother in being most obvious.

"I say, sir," Thomas remarked. "How will we shake off that log? There is too much moss upon it. Do you think pixies live in the moss?"

"We will find out when we come back for it," Grafton said. "We have to dust it off thoroughly before bringing it inside. I do not want wild pixies running about and ruining my mother's preparations. Once they make it inside, it's a devil of a time getting them back out."

Grafton remembered the tales his tutor had indulged him with when he was Thomas' age. Christmas pixies wishing to invade a human home to celebrate and make merry mayhem was one of Grafton's favorites.

His father had rarely come home for Christmas, so his mother started the tradition of inviting various friends for the holiday. Robbie and his parents were guests every year. They were the best attempt at *family* he had truly known.

"Be careful, Thomas. We do not know how the wee folk of Warwickshire behave," Lucinda said. Then she laughed, and Grafton was again enchanted by the sound. She was much more animated around her siblings. He was quite glad they had come. Their lighthearted warmth was a welcome diversion from dire thoughts of catching a killer.

Grafton pretended offense. "Madam, do you imply the wee folk here are more mischievous than those at Bronley Manor?"

"But of course. We have had no problems with our Yule log, have we, Thomas?" Lucinda said.

"None at all," Miss Bethany and Miss Margaret chimed in together, then dissolved into a fit of giggles.

Thomas made a face, knowing his sisters teased him. He followed Grafton to an evergreen and held his arms wide to catch the cut boughs.

As Thomas loaded the wagon with fragrant branches, Grafton watched the ladies gather up holly. Their cheeks and noses were rosy red. Lucinda looked relaxed. Her smile was warm and her laughter contagious. He watched her as if entranced by a meadow nymph. At first he did not hear Thomas' question.

"Do we need more boughs, sir?"

"Yes, of course." He turned his attention back to snipping the evergreen branches, and then he heard a shot.

"Oh!" Lucinda gasped.

Grafton's heart sank when he saw her grab her arm. He was at her side in a trice. "What is it?" Then he saw the blood. She had been shot, on his land! He pulled his handkerchief out of his pocket. "Let me see." He inspected the small wound and found it merely a graze. Even so, he wrapped the linen around her upper arm.

"It cannot be bad. It simply stings," she said. But her lips trembled.

Her sisters had gathered around her. "What happened?" Bethany's eyes were round with fright.

Grafton looked into Lucinda's eyes. Knowing she would rather not alarm her family, he made up the most logical explanation. "A poacher looking for his Christmas dinner. Now everyone into the wagon and stay low until I check the grounds."

Lucinda gave him a grateful nod. "I am fine, truly." She did not look fine. Her face was as pale as a white sheet.

Even so, he gave her hands a quick squeeze. "Thomas, stay here with your sisters, and keep your heads down. I shall be only a moment." He darted off to where he thought the shot had come from but knew it was of no use. His *poacher* was long gone.

He wished with all his might his fib was true and there was no killer lurking in their midst, trying to harm Lucinda. He searched the area but there was no trace of anyone and he dared not leave the Bronwells alone and unprotected.

When he returned, Lucinda's sisters had wrapped her in blankets. She looked small and helpless. The joy of the Christmas activity had been knocked firmly out of him and he seethed with fury.

Good God! Again someone had hurt her with him looking on. His hands clenched into fists. Who would dare come onto his land? He was determined to find out.

Once again, Lucinda found herself in bed and fussed over. Her arm had only been nicked and the wound felt no worse than a very bad scrape, except that it throbbed. She wanted to help decorate the hall, but her mother forbade her to get up before dinner. At least she would not miss that too.

A soft knock at the door caught her attention. "Come in."

Lord Grafton entered her room, leaving the door open. "May I?"

She sat up straighter and her hand tucked at the knot of her hair. "Of course."

He sat in the chair near her bed. "I beg your pardon for disturbing you, but I needed to make sure you were all right. Your mother said you would heal up just fine, but . . ." Deep lines showed around the corners of his eyes. He ran a hand through his hair. "I am so sorry that this happened."

"Goodness, 'tis not your fault." She pulled the covers tighter. "And the wound is just a scratch, really."

"To think this happened on my lands." His lips thinned to a hard line.

"Perhaps it was merely a poacher as you said." But she did not quite believe it either. Had she not bent down to pick up a dropped sprig of holly at that very moment— She shuddered to think where the bullet might have hit her.

He shook his head. "You know as well as I that it wasn't. I returned with my men to search for the culprit and bring home the Yule log. There was no evidence of someone hunting. We found the tracks of a lone horse, but no footprints. The rider did not bother to dismount."

She shivered with shock that someone wanted to shoot her, kill her.

"I also wished to beg a favor." His worried expression tore at her heart.

"Yes?"

"Please do not come downstairs this evening. There will be so many people coming and going. I fear I cannot properly protect you."

Disappointment swamped her. She so wanted to attend.

He reached out and cupped her chin. "Please stay here, where I know you will be safe. In fact, I would feel a deal better if your entire family remained with you tonight."

The warmth of his hand radiated through her. In his eyes, she read the concern and worry he carried for her. She felt herself nod before realizing she would do whatever he asked of her. "What of the house party?"

He let go and stood. "Unfortunately, I need to judge our guests as they interact with you, but I am sorely tempted to lock you away somewhere and keep you safe."

She nodded. Being locked away would not be such a bad thing if he were there with her.

"Robbie will arrive tonight and he will help. One of us will accompany you everywhere. Lady Anne knows there is a mystery afoot, and she will watch over Thomas and Miss Margaret with efficiency."

Again she nodded. The realization of the danger she had exposed her family to settled in the pit of her stomach and soured it.

"You must rest and get well." His gaze bore into hers. "We have a trying twelve days ahead of us, but I promise, I will find the man responsible."

She was encouraged by the look of steely determination in his eyes, taking comfort in his resolve. He would protect her—of that, she felt certain. "I know you will find him, my lord."

He looked as if he wished to say something more, but instead, he nodded and left through the open door.

Chapter Nine

*G*rafton left Lucinda's room, feeling helpless and very much like he had failed her. He saw the fear that had lurked behind her wide blue eyes regardless of how brave she tried to be. He had wanted to take her into his arms, but he could hardly do so in her bedchamber, in her very bed, no less. It was not at all the thing for him to visit her there, but he had to see her—make certain she would recover.

For once in his life, he did not care about appearances. Lucinda was in real danger and he had invited the threat into his home. He hoped he had done the right thing. But what if he had just opened Pandora's box?

He went to his study, where he found Robbie waiting for him.

"You look like hell," Robbie said.

"Nice to see you too." Grafton poured brandy for the both of them. He needed one.

"How is your lovely widow?" He winked.

"Recovering from a gunshot wound she received today."

Robbie was out of his seat. "You're joking."

"Do I look like I am?"

"God's breath, you're serious. What happened?"

"We were gathering holly in the woods between Ivy Park and here when all of a sudden a bullet tore through the air and grazed her upper arm."

Robbie fell back into his chair. "But she will recover."

"Yes. The doctor said it is only a nick. She will be fine, but I cannot say the same for me. Robbie, this happened on my land. The guests do not arrive until tomorrow, but the Darrows live only five miles away. They must know about the open house tonight and that we'd be out gathering greens."

Robbie scratched his chin. "And guess who I ran into while I took my luncheon at the Rose and Slipper?"

"Who?"

"The angry Mr. Lewes."

Grafton bolted for the door. "What are we waiting for? Let us go there this instant."

"Just a moment," Robbie said. "We cannot act rashly."

"What time did you see Lewes?" Grafton asked.

" 'Twas nearly noon."

"Plenty of time for the scoundrel to ride hard from the inn and wait in the field for Lucinda."

Robbie raised his hands and gestured for him to calm down. "There is no proof or hint of evidence that would verify it was Mr. Lewes. How would he even know where you would be? Surely he would not have had enough time to scour the fields to find you."

"He could easily have heard us. We were not a quiet lot."

Robbie rubbed his chin. "No, I suspect not. But after checking into his background, I can say there is nothing the least bit unsavory about him."

Grafton did not wish to hear such news. "He has the most to gain and he was furious at the reading of Sir Alaric's will. He swore he would contest it." Grafton was champing at the bit to do something. Today's accident had shaken him to the core. "The girth to Lady Darrow's saddle had been cut while Mr. Lewes was at Ivy Park, and now another accident has happened while he was nearby."

"All true. Also true is the fact that Mr. Lewes has filed a complaint with his solicitor—he has already taken the steps to contest, hardly the action of a man bent on murder. I believe it is in our best interest to wait until he is under your roof. If he is our man, he will no doubt try again."

"And that puts Lucinda at risk."

"Indeed." Robbie scratched his head. "We could go to the magistrate with what we have, but if Mr. Lewes is not to blame, we risk publicly accusing an innocent man with mere hearsay and ruining his reputation."

Grafton sat back down. Robbie was right. Grafton wanted the hard truth. He could not jump to conclusions just yet.

"These threats may not be motivated by money," Robbie said. "The family could be acting out of spite. Your lovely widow did take a large amount away from Sir Alaric's nephew. Perhaps these incidents are meant to scare her rather than actually kill her."

Grafton shook his head. It was little comfort, especially since he had witnessed how hard Lucinda fell from Ariel. There was sense in Robbie's words, however. Robbie's reference to Lucinda as Grafton's *own* struck an odd chord within him. His heart warmed at the thought of her belonging to him. He firmly put those tempting thoughts aside. Now was not the time to languish over her like a lovesick poet.

A scratch at the door interrupted. "Yes?"

His mother peeked in. "Dougie, many of our tenants have arrived and are asking for you."

"Forgive me. I have neglected my duties as host." He turned to Robbie. "You are welcome to dine at our open house, or if you prefer privacy, a tray can be arranged."

Robbie also stood. "The open house will be fine. Perhaps one of your tenants saw someone this afternoon. I shall see what I can find out."

Grafton flashed a quick glance at his mother. She knew he had invented the poacher story told earlier, but she promised to remain quiet. He slapped his friend on the back. "Very good."

The next morning Lucinda woke to the sound of church bells announcing Christmas Day. Ice appeared on her windows and she leapt out of bed to see if it had snowed. To her disappointment, it had not, but a blanket of glittering frost covered the ground. The temperature had dipped drastically overnight, making the grounds sparkle in the winter sunshine like a fairy kingdom.

Her family had joined her in her bedchamber last

night. Lord Grafton had graciously decided to forgo the tradition of lighting the Yule log until Christmas Day so that they might all enjoy the custom. That had bolstered Thomas' spirits immensely.

Trays laden with samples of the food served in the great hall had been sent to her room and they had enjoyed a merry feast. Lucinda had sat near the fire with her family to play a rousing game of loo, and then they had made paper chains to wrap around the greenery while their mother worked at her needlepoint.

Coming away from the window, Lucinda washed and donned a warm black gown of merino wool with black lace along the square neckline. It was one of the new gowns from the nearby village and would serve her well.

When the maid finished styling her hair in a classic upsweep, Lucinda left her bedchamber. She headed for the breakfast room, where she knew she would find Lord Grafton. But when she entered, he was not alone.

"Happy Christmas, Lord Grafton," she said.

"Happy Christmas to you." Lord Grafton stood, as did the young man seated next to him. "Lucinda, may I present to you my good friend and solicitor, Mr. Robert Sinclair."

Lucinda bowed. "Nice to meet you, Mr. Sinclair."

He openly stared at her before realizing his error. "Lady Darrow, a pleasure." Mr. Sinclair waited until she was seated. "May I fill your plate?"

"Please. Eggs and some ham, I think." She glanced at Lord Grafton. "How was your open house?"

"Very fine. Tell Thomas we did not thoroughly dust the Yule log before bringing it in. We can light it this afternoon, before the guests arrive."

She smiled. "He shall be so excited. It was all he could talk of last night." Mr. Sinclair placed a plate in front of her.

"Thank you for remaining in your chamber," Lord Grafton said. "My mind was relieved knowing you were safe. Robbie did some nosing about and one of my tenants did see a man on horseback, but unfortunately he did not get a good look at the chap, so we have no idea who it might have been."

Lucinda looked at Mr. Sinclair.

"You can speak freely, Lady Darrow." Mr. Sinclair took a sip of his coffee. "Grafton has apprised me of the situation. These past weeks I have been looking into the backgrounds of each and every person who inherited from Sir Alaric."

"And did you find the Bronwell history satisfactory then?"

Lord Grafton had the grace to color slightly. "Indeed, it was."

"Might you share this information with me?" She wanted to know what she was dealing with this coming week and who to look out for.

Mr. Sinclair looked at Lord Grafton, who nodded for him to go ahead. "So much of it is sketchy at best, but Sir Leonard is up to his eyeballs in debt. The funds he inherited will hardly cover it. There is very little information on his wife, Sylvia Harris. A common enough name and her parents were listed as dead in the church register on their wedding day. Lady Willow sponsored her come-out in Bath, where

Miss Harris was introduced to Sir Leonard, but that is all we know.

"Sir Leonard's sisters each married well and have seen little hardship. Both of their husbands are of sterling character and sound income.

"Mr. Lewes, as you know, needs the shares you possess as collateral for a loan to recoup his recent investment and shipping losses. He is, at present, low on funds." Mr. Sinclair took a deep breath. "Which leaves us with Lady Willow, Sir Alaric's longtime mistress." He looked quickly at her and added, "I beg your pardon."

"I already know, Mr. Sinclair," Lucinda said. "Pray continue."

"Sir Alaric and Lord Willow fought a duel over Lady Willow and Lord Willow lost. An agreement was made between the men, and Lord Willow signed over all of his business shares to Sir Alaric. Now, as you heard at the reading of the will, Lady Willow received those shares back.

"Lord Willow became sickly after the duel and died within months in a carriage accident. Lady Willow mourned the appropriate amount of time before heading to Bath with Miss Harris—now Sir Leonard's wife. There is nothing else out of the ordinary to be found."

"Did Sir Alaric resume his affair with Lady Willow?" Lucinda asked.

"Frankly, I do not know." Mr. Sinclair looked at Lord Grafton. "Had you heard anything while you were in Town?"

Lord Grafton shrugged. "Unfortunately, I knew only of the duel that resulted from their affair. I did

not hear any gossip about the two of them re-
newing it."

"Well, she has nothing more to gain, and truly,
neither do the Darrows. But Mr. Lewes . . ." Lucinda
looked at Lord Grafton. "What do you think?"

"I think that for the entirety of the holiday you
cannot allow yourself or any of your family to be
alone with any of them. Do not go out of doors without Robbie or myself."

The dire nature of the situation fell upon her shoul-
ders like of cape of lead. "What of my family? Surely
I will be safe with my mother, my sisters, or even
Lady Grafton."

Lord Grafton looked thoughtful. "Perhaps a quick
pass in the courtyard with your family."

She nodded her agreement. It was only twelve
days. She could withstand being caged in at Arden
Hall to lessen the danger. Regardless, she planned to
stay far away from Mr. Lewes.

The door opened and Bethany, Margaret, and
Thomas entered, followed by Lady Anne.

"Good morning," Bethany said. "And Happy
Christmas."

Mr. Sinclair stood immediately, nearly knocking
over his chair.

Lord Grafton actually chuckled, but he stood as
well. "Miss Bethany, Miss Margaret, and Master
Thomas, may I introduce my good friend, Mr. Sinclair? Robbie, the Misses Bronwell and their brother.
You know Lady Anne."

Bethany curtsied and blushed profusely. "Pleased
to make your acquaintance, sir."

Lucinda noticed that Mr. Sinclair was a bit tongue-tied and his color was heightened. She quickly glanced at Bethany, who peeked at him from beneath lowered lashes.

"Might I fill your plate, Miss Bronwell?" said Mr. Sinclair, finding his manners.

"Indeed."

"I shall get my own, thank you," Margaret said, then added, "And Thomas' too." She followed an amused Lady Anne to the sideboard.

Lucinda tried not to smile. "Very good, Margaret," she whispered. But she watched Bethany, now seated, as she demurely poured a cup of tea and waited for Mr. Sinclair's offering. Lucinda looked up in time to catch Lord Grafton's gaze. He inquisitively lifted a dark eyebrow.

Lucinda frowned. She knew what their mother would think. She would not wish Bethany's head turned before she had the chance to go to London for a Season. Lucinda agreed, for Bethany might enjoy Town in a way Lucinda never could. Until then, her sister was far too young for a courtship. She had never even been in the company of gentlemen before. Perhaps they should rethink her attendance with the adults during the holiday party. But that would break her heart, and Lucinda knew neither she nor her mother could do that.

"We made paper chains last night, my lord," Thomas said after he swallowed a mouthful of eggs.

"Did you?"

"Bethany thought of it. We are going to hang them after we break our fast." Thomas grinned. "And then can we light the Yule log?"

Grafton glanced at Lucinda, who nodded. "I think

that would be an excellent time." He poured another cup of coffee. His meal had long since been eaten but he was in no hurry to leave. In fact, despite the fact that his house would soon be filled with unwanted guests, for now, he relaxed. He wanted to savor the moment for as long as he possibly could.

He leaned back and sipped his steaming brew, enjoying the festive sound of the Bronwell family chatter. Used to eating his breakfast alone, he had adjusted to Lucinda's presence most mornings. Her family was a welcome addition, and they would indeed help protect her.

He wished the house party to the devil, but knew he might never again have the chance to uncover the killer. He could hardly keep Lucinda at Arden Hall forever, or could he? His heart did a somersault at the thought. His mother had planted the seed that Lucinda might make an agreeable bride. The absurdity of the idea had long since worn off, leaving him to ponder if perhaps it was not quite so far-fetched as he first thought.

When young Thomas finally had eaten his fill, and Robbie had waited upon the lovely Miss Bethany enough times to make the girl blush, they departed the coziness of the breakfast room for the wide-open space of the great hall, which was decorated with evergreens and holly and bows. The Bronwell ladies departed to fetch their paper chains and their mother. Lady Anne had gone to her rooms for a warm shawl, and Grafton, Thomas, and Robbie stood before the massive Yule log, which lay next to the huge hearth swept clean from last night's fire.

"Shall we lift it in?" Grafton asked Robbie.

Robbie took off his jacket and rolled up his sleeves. Thomas followed suit.

"Very well, then." Grafton took off his jacket and helped the two move the log into position.

"Did you check for the pixies?" Thomas asked.

"While we wait for the ladies' return, you may wish to inspect the moss further. Make sure no wee folk were missed."

Thomas' blue eyes grew as wide as saucers, but he hurried to check the log.

Grafton reached against the far wall for the bell rope. When his housekeeper entered the hall, he asked that she bring in a bowl of spiced ale posset. "To give us something with which to toast the log," he explained when he noticed Robbie's look of surprise.

"I had no idea you were fond of such traditions," Robbie said quietly. "You used to leave the log and even the greenery to the servants."

"This year is different." It was. The Bronwells had brought a sense of family to Arden Hall and, with that, an enjoyment of otherwise empty traditions.

Robbie's eyes narrowed. "I should say so."

Grafton was in no mood to discuss the reason and was glad his friend kept quiet. Lucinda made the difference and they both knew it.

The young ladies joined them with yards of colored paper rings and golden cord. Never before had he looked forward to such a simple task. Despite the chill in the room from the cold hearth, the laughter and holiday spirit warmed him. The anticipation in young Thomas' face alone was worth holding off the lighting of the Yule log until today.

"My lord, are they even?" Lucinda stood on a stool fetched from the kitchens. She had twined the colorful paper creations around the swags of evergreen and ivy sprigged with holly.

"I would say so." But he hardly noticed the chains. He watched her every graceful moment. Her wound gave her some trouble when she tried to raise her arm, but she managed without a whimper. The mourning gown of black wool that she wore did not disguise her slender figure or full bosom. He could not help but admire her shape as she leaned to tuck gold cord into place.

"Oh, how lovely." His mother entered the hall with Mrs. Bronwell and Lady Anne. They were followed by Mrs. Smith, the housekeeper, delivering the posset. "Lucinda, what a nice touch."

"Thank you, but it was Bethany's idea."

That young woman stood next to Robbie, and the two appeared to be in a world of their own making. Miss Bethany did not hear the compliment paid by her sister. Mrs. Bronwell took a decided interest in this development and headed toward the two immediately.

"It appears my sister is quite taken with your solicitor," Lucinda said quietly when she stood next to Grafton and surveyed her work.

"He is a good man."

"No doubt."

"But not what you hope for your sister?" Did she think Robbie beneath their notice now that she was a rich heiress?

She looked him straight in the eye. "Not at all, sir. Marriage to Sir Alaric secured dowries for both

Bethany and Margaret. They need never look for anything less than love."

Properly corrected, he realized that he felt safer
thinking of her as a fortune hunter. "Then why the
concern?" he asked.

"Bethany is only seventeen. She lacks experience
with gentlemen. In fact, she has met very few."

Grafton thought he understood. Considering the
experience Lucinda had had with gentleman these
past two Seasons, he should not begrudge her protec-
tiveness. "I shall place a word of caution in Robbie's ears."

"Thank you." She moved close to her mother and
whispered in her ear, no doubt informing Mrs. Bronwell of what he had just offered.

A tug on his sleeve broke his thoughts. "What can
I do for you, Master Thomas?"

"The Yule log, sir. The chains have all been hung."

He ruffled the lad's hair. "Indeed they are. And
you have checked the log's moss?"

"Thoroughly, sir. There are no wee folk present."

"Very well. Then let us proceed," Grafton
announced.

With great pomp, they observed the tradition of
lighting the giant log that would be kept burning
until Twelfth Night. He gave the boy the honor of
catching the log with a fiery tinder stick left from
last year's log.

Young Thomas took his duty seriously and walked
carefully to the hearth. Slowly, he bent and caught
the tinder to the kindling they arranged. When the
bark of the Yule log caught fire, the group burst forth
with applause.

Grafton lifted his mug of posset. "I toast this log that it will burn brightly for the twelve days of Christmas and warm us with its heat."

"Hear, hear," Robbie said.

They raised their mugs, then sat down to sip away the sweet ale and enjoy the crackling fire before them.

"Goodness, look at the time." Grafton's mother jumped to her feet. "The guests will arrive soon and I have yet to check the room assignments."

"May we help?" Lucinda asked.

His mother smiled. "Come, let us see what is left to be done."

The women left the great hall chattering on about last-minute details.

Grafton remained behind with Robbie and Thomas, and the three of them whiled away the afternoon with stories of hunting and the recounting of memories. When Grafton and Robbie began reminiscing about pranks they played as schoolboys, Thomas laughed heartily, and Grafton knew they had given the lad ideas to take back to school.

Lucinda might scold him for teaching her little brother such antics, but he would wager that she would be grateful too that he had included Thomas.

It did not cease to amaze him how quickly his thoughts turned to Lucinda. She was always there, simmering just below the surface of his daily duties. He would not soon forget the vision of her twining paper chains around the swags of evergreen. Her concentration had been fixed firmly upon her task, giving him the opportunity to watch her without her knowledge of him doing so.

He skated on thin ice by allowing this fascination with her to grow into something stronger than he wanted to admit. Part of him did not care. Perhaps it was time he thought about what he wanted rather than what he thought he should attain.

He drained his mug of posset. As much as he wished this cozy reprieve might go on indefinitely, he had guests coming and a murderer to catch.

Chapter Ten

*L*ucinda took utmost care in dressing for dinner. She sat before the vanity, looking into the mirror, as the maid arranged her hair. She fidgeted with the clasp of Alaric's pearls, her fingers running along the strand to stop at the tiny metal clip. Over and over she played with the necklace.

"You'll break it, ma'am, if you keep at it."

"Yes, of course." She firmly clasped her hands in her lap.

The guests had trickled in like raindrops throughout the afternoon. Sir Leonard's sisters, Mrs. Lindley and Mrs. Wakeham, arrived with their husbands. Each woman had brought a mountain of luggage and their own ladies' maid.

Lucinda remembered Lord Grafton's expression when the guests began to fill the house and nearly laughed. His face had gone completely pale when he realized the extent of the Lindley-Wakeham storm that had descended upon Arden Hall.

With a quick knock, Bethany peeked her head into Lucinda's room. "Are you ready?"

Lucinda looked anxiously in the mirror. She worried that the neckline of her new gown might offend Lord Grafton. It was completely decent, nearly modest, but her form was not easily hidden and this dress pushed up her breasts until they swelled above the lace-edged neckline.

Lucinda turned around to face her mother, who had entered behind Bethany. "Do you think this dress too fast for mourning?"

Her mother smiled. "You look beautiful, my dear."

Lucinda splayed her fingers across her chest. "Not too low?"

"Goodness, Lucy. You are not in a convent," Bethany chirped.

Lucinda tipped her head and took in the vision of her sister. Bethany looked terribly grown-up in a light gray gown of soft silk with a silvery sheen. They shared the maid Lady Grafton had assigned, and the girl had done wonders with Bethany's thick thatch of dark blond hair. Fortunately Bethany's figure had not blossomed the way Lucinda's had. "And you, Beth, are stunning."

A deep blush stole over her sister's cheeks.

Lucinda hoped Lord Grafton had talked with Mr. Sinclair, because one look at her sleek and sophisticated sister and the man was bound to be lost.

"We must hurry, Lucinda," her mother said. "I do not wish to be the last ones to the drawing room."

"Of course." Lucinda fingered the pearls Alaric had given her. She hoped they took the focus away from her bosom.

They were hardly the last to enter the drawing room, but even so, Lucinda felt every pair of eyes boring through her. She managed to raise her chin a notch and boldly meet each look with her head held high. She wondered who among them tried to hurt her. A surge of fury pulsed through her and she managed to cast a look of contempt toward Mr. Lewes, who stood near the fireplace.

She glanced at Lord Grafton, who nodded his approval, and Lucinda felt further encouraged—and relieved. He did not appear displeased with her gown.

The introductions were again made and Mr. Lewes approached her with a pleasant expression. He bowed over her hand and he whispered, "I must humbly beg your forgiveness for the last time we met. I was beyond rude."

"It was a difficult time for all of us." She lifted her chin.

"Indeed, but still, I appreciate your graciousness, Dowager."

Lucinda nodded.

He moved along and was soon replaced by Sir Leonard and Lady Darrow. "How well you look, Lucinda," Lady Darrow gushed. "I must declare that mourning suits you. I could never abide dark colors. But on you, my dear, they look divine. You can wear black."

"Thank you," Lucinda said.

Sir Leonard bowed and mumbled something unintelligible.

The Lindleys and the Wakehams arrived and then finally Lady Willow made a grand entrance. The elegant widow headed straight for Lucinda.

"My dear Dowager Lady Darrow." She grasped Lucinda's hands. "We finally meet under more lighthearted circumstances. How are you holding up through all of this? How generous of Lord Grafton to open his home and bring us all together again, even in our grief."

Lucinda looked into Lady Willow's kind face. It was not hard to believe the lady had been Alaric's mistress. Lucinda saw real sadness in the older woman's lovely brown eyes. It was obvious she had truly cared for Alaric, and despite the impropriety of her actions, Lucinda's heart went out to her. "I am managing just fine."

"Of course you are." Lady Willow patted her hands. "Dowager is much too old for you. May I call you Lucinda?"

Lucinda smiled. "You may." There was something very warm and inviting about Lady Willow. It was no wonder Alaric had been enamored of her. Lucinda watched the elegant widow float away to speak with Lady Grafton.

"Please remember what I told you." Lord Grafton had come up to stand beside her.

She had not heard him draw near, since she was watching Lady Willow. "Sir?"

"Do not go anywhere alone." His voice was low— whispered for her ears alone.

She shivered, despite the warmth of the room. "I have no desire to put myself in harm's way," she whispered back.

He gave her elbow an encouraging squeeze, and then Naughton announced dinner.

Once seated at the head of the large dining table in the great hall, Grafton gave his mother, seated at the opposite end, a nod. Dinner could be served. Conversation quieted as the footmen brought forth tureens of soup and the first course.

Grafton watched as Lucinda leaned back to be served. She had impressed him. Instead of cowering when she first entered the drawing room, she stood firm, commanding respect with a direct gaze. He had worried about how she might handle the guests, but his fears had been firmly put to rest when she stared down Mr. Lewes. Lucinda Bronwell was no shrinking violet. But of course, he knew that. She was far more than he had ever bargained for.

She wore the pearls Sir Alaric had given her and her fingers touched them often. Her graceful neck needed no adornment, nor did the expanse of creamy skin above the bodice of her gown. His gaze kept straying there, every time she touched those dratted pearls!

He forced his focus elsewhere and surveyed his guests seated around the table. Mr. Lewes remained on his best behavior with no angry outbursts. For whatever reason, Lady Darrow was rather quiet. She scarcely spoke unless spoken to, which he found odd. Sir Leonard chatted happily with one of his brothers-in-law, Mr. Lindley, he thought. Lady Willow softened the entire group with her polished grace and Town bronze. Not one person looked or acted like a murderer. They were off to an interesting start.

For Mrs. Bronwell's sake, as well as Robbie's concentration, he had placed Miss Bethany farther down the table, close to his mother. He needed his friend's perceptive manner at work with no distractions. Fortunately, Robbie had not taken offense when Grafton cautioned him toward Lucinda's sister. In fact, Robbie had already judged Miss Bethany too young to encourage and promised to tread with care.

The slack drop of Robbie's jaw when he first beheld Miss Bethany, however, said little for his prudence. He had looked like a man enraptured. But Grafton trusted him and knew Robbie would never lead Miss Bethany astray or toward heartache.

The youngest Bronwells, Miss Margaret and young Thomas, were safely tucked in the nursery. Lady Anne promised to keep them out of sight for now at least.

The meal progressed and the chatter turned toward the weather. The evening had turned very cold and they all wondered if their holiday would be graced by snow. After the bowl of nuts and fruit had made its rounds, Grafton's mother stood and announced that the ladies would leave the men to their port.

A relaxed atmosphere settled amid the pouring of spirits.

"I say, my lord, dashed nice of you to invite us all together for the holidays." Sir Leonard nodded for the footman to fill his glass a little fuller.

Grafton leaned back in his chair. "Seemed like a good idea, considering you were newly installed at Ivy Park. After the tragedy of Sir Alaric's death, I thought it appropriate to honor his absence with a gathering reminiscent of one of his own."

"My uncle did love a holiday," Sir Leonard said. "Used to invite half the *ton* to Ivy Park."

Grafton sipped his brandy. "Indeed." He had attended few of those gatherings with his mother. Unfortunately there were several men who attended each year who he did not want near her, with their leering and lustful ways. Grafton's father and Sir Alaric had cried friends, which meant they both ran with a dangerously lascivious crowd. Even so, his father rarely pulled himself away from London, even at Christmas.

"Sir Alaric was a man with a head for business," Mr. Lewes added as he savored his port thoughtfully.

The mood turned solemn and each man recounted a memory of Sir Alaric. A fitting tribute, but Grafton watched them closely as they delivered their speeches. He could not detect from one of them any gladness that the man was dead. Even Sir Leonard, who had everything to gain by coming into the title, displayed genuine sentimentality when he spoke of his departed uncle.

Grafton glanced at Robbie, who raised his eyebrow in bewilderment. Not one of these men gave away any clues.

The ladies headed for the drawing room but Lucinda and her mother lagged behind. Bethany walked beside Lady Grafton and the two discussed how prettily the gold rope adorning the paper chains twinkled in the candlelight. The other women bunched in between, chatting about the meal.

Lucinda's mother whispered close to her ear, "I do believe I have seen Lady Darrow with Lady Willow before."

"At the funeral, perhaps?"

"Before that."

"In Bath? Lady Willow sponsored her come-out."

"I do not know for sure, but I shall try to remember."

Lucinda looked at her mother's furrowed brow and patted her hand. "I am certain that you will."

She had not told her mother the real reason for her *accidents*. Her arm still throbbed with a dull ache but she refused to mention it to her mother, who had been through so much the past few years that her health had suffered. Her mother could worry herself into illness and land in bed for weeks. Lucinda could not allow that to happen when Arden Hall was filled with guests. Her hosts had enough to worry over and her mother needn't become an added concern.

They entered the drawing room, which was decorated for Christmas with greenery and red ribbon. Flames from a large fire danced with sizzles and snaps behind the grate. Lucinda made sure her mother sat close to the hearth for warmth.

"Lucinda, do join us for a game of whist." Lady Willow sat at a table with Mrs. Lindley and Lady Darrow.

Lucinda turned to her mother. "Bethany will join you in a moment."

"No matter, go on and play," said her mother.

Lucinda took her place across from Lady Willow, who dealt. "Please, ladies, do call me Lucinda. It will lessen the confusion since there are two Lady Darrows present."

"A splendid idea." Lady Willow smiled as she cut the deck and handed one card to each of them.

Mrs. Wakeham pulled a chair close to her sister,

Mrs. Lindley. "Do go on with your game. I wish only to watch," she said quickly, then added, " 'Lucinda' is such a pretty name."

Her words were nice, but Lucinda did not mistake Mrs. Wakeham's sneer when she spoke.

"I almost named my daughter that, but Charles hated the name. He preferred Elizabeth," Mrs. Lindley said. "More royal tradition and all that."

Lucinda ignored Mrs. Lindley's jab and smiled politely. She gathered up her card and flipped it over—a jack of hearts.

"We shall be partners." Lady Willow nodded toward Lucinda. They had the two highest cards. Lady Willow scooped up the deck and dealt again, then turned over the last card to determine trump. "Diamonds. How lovely."

The women fanned their cards in their hands, arranging and rearranging them according to suit until finally they were ready. Lucinda noticed that Mrs. Lindley and Mrs. Wakeham shared several pointed glances and barely controlled titters.

"I shall go first," Mrs. Lindley said as she laid down a low club.

Lucinda played a three of diamonds. She looked up at Lady Willow, wishing she could convey that her hand was full of trump and little else.

"My dear Lucinda, you may have laid trump but I will take the trick. I have a five of diamonds and will take your place to lead," Lady Darrow said.

Lucinda cringed. Lady Darrow had indeed taken her place as mistress of Ivy Park. Had she poisoned Alaric to make that possible? Lady Darrow's cheeks suddenly reddened as if she had read Lucinda's thoughts.

An awkward hush settled over the table. Lucinda wondered what the other ladies were thinking. A prolonged silence only added to the tension until finally Lady Willow spoke. "Lucinda, did you know that my late husband and yours were bosom bows?" She took the trick with a ten of diamonds.

"Indeed." Should Lucinda let on that she knew there was far more to it than that?

"They were quite the best of friends who got up to any manner of mischief. 'Tis how I met Sir Alaric—my husband introduced us."

The fact that Lady Willow should become the mistress of her husband's dearest friend was indeed repulsive. But her perfect manners, kindness, and depth of feeling where Alaric was concerned somehow softened her dishonor.

"I see," said Lucinda.

Lady Willow led with a king of hearts. "He was a ripping gallant in his day, but of course he remained so for years. 'Tis no wonder you married him. Regardless of age, Sir Alaric never lost his charm."

Lucinda saw the bittersweet sadness in Lady Willow's eyes once again. She must have loved Alaric.

"A surprise that he married." Mrs. Lindley played her card. "Sir Alaric was a confirmed bachelor after all."

"A testimony to Lucinda's charm," Lady Willow said and nodded her approval when Lucinda laid down her card. "Do make your play, Lady Darrow."

Lady Darrow shuffled her cards. "A pity he hadn't

married earlier." Lady Willow cast Lady Darrow an odd look. Lady Darrow nervously played her card. "That is to say—well, one can only wonder why he avoided matrimony for so long."

Lady Willow won the trick again and smiled triumphantly. "He had not found the right woman, until he met Lucinda."

"Of course," Lady Darrow hurriedly agreed.

"Indeed," Mrs. Lindley added.

Perhaps the ladies thought they were being polite, but the truth of the matter was that they clearly thought Lucinda had coerced Alaric into marrying her. She would wager that none of them, including Lady Willow, believed the nonsense that spilled from their lips.

They continued to play and Lady Willow entertained them with the latest gossip from Town. Not another word was uttered about Sir Alaric, and Lucinda was relieved. Lady Willow and Lucinda beat Lady Darrow and Mrs. Lindley soundly. They were about to begin another round when the timely arrival of the gentlemen interrupted them.

"Nothing like a game of whist," Mr. Lewes said.

"Please, take my place." Lucinda got up from the table. She had wearied of the game, but more so, she was tired of the company.

"Here, Mr. Lindley." Lady Willow stood. "You may have my place and partner your wife. I have a surprise I must first discuss with Lady Grafton."

"I love surprises," Mrs. Wakeham said with a clap of her hands.

"Of course you do, dearest," her sister, Mrs. Lindley, said.

Lucinda stood behind the settee, surveying the room, when she noticed Lord Grafton coming toward her.

"You look tired," he said softly. "Is your arm giving you trouble?"

She looked up into his concerned face. "Not at all." Lucinda was not about to confess that she had wearied of the company already. How she wished they could have celebrated the holiday alone, just her family and Grafton's, but she held her tongue. Her presence here was only a matter of circumstance. It was not as if she had been invited to Arden Hall.

Lady Grafton stood and asked for attention, and the guests quieted.

Alarmed, Lucinda glanced at Lord Grafton, who shrugged his shoulders. He obviously had no idea what his mother was up to.

"Ladies and gentlemen, in the spirit of Christmas, Lady Willow has graciously brought small gifts for a delightful game of surprise. If you all will make a circle with your chairs, Lady Willow will share the rules of the game."

Lucinda relaxed. She noticed that Lord Grafton did too.

While the gentlemen arranged the chairs, Lady Willow sent a servant on an errand. The footman returned with a large velvet sack filled with beribboned boxes.

"Oh, what fun," Lady Darrow said, but her gaze strayed toward her husband. Sir Leonard slouched in his chair, oblivious to the revelry surrounding him. He appeared to be under the influence of too much port.

With the help of the footman, Lady Willow handed out a box to each person before she made her way to the pianoforte. "This game is quite amusing. When you hear me sing the word 'love,' you must hand your gift to the person on your right repeatedly until you hear me sing the word 'love' once again, and then you must hand your gifts to the person on your left repeatedly.

"Every time I sing the word 'love,' you must switch direction. When the song is over, the gifts are then opened."

Lucinda looked at her sister Bethany, who sat next to Mr. Sinclair. She rattled her box and giggled when Mr. Sinclair put his box to his ear. It was a jolly way to pass the evening. Even Mr. Lewes looked cheerful.

Lady Willow played the pianoforte, singing an age-old song of love and heartbreak. The dramatic tale was lost to the hilarity of the game. Quickly, they passed the gifts to their right and then their left, laughing when someone could not keep up or dropped a box.

Lucinda sat next to Lord Grafton and her weariness disappeared the moment she heard his laughter. Several times as they passed a gift, their fingers became intertwined, which only served to make them both laugh harder.

After several minutes had passed, the song wound to a close. Lady Willow drew out the final notes and said the word "love" one last time.

Lord Grafton handed Lucinda her gift—a box larger than the others and tied with gold ribbon. "Open it," he said with merry gray eyes.

She looked around as others tore into their gifts.

The air filled with gasps of delight and laughter when a treasured trinket was revealed. Snuffboxes, handkerchiefs, quizzing glasses, and even some clever toys were unwrapped to the amusement of all.

Lucinda slowly untied the bow of her box under the watchful eyes of all the other guests, who had already torn through their gifts. She stopped when Lord Grafton opened his box and found a pair of warm wool mittens. "Those will be most welcome this week," she said.

"Open yours."

Excitement raced through her. She pushed the ribbon out of her way and opened the box. With a startled gasp, she saw brightly colored eyes painted on the toy inside the box stare back at her. She bent closer and the toy literally sprang to life, hitting her squarely in the eye.

"Oh!" She covered her eye and the box fell from her lap to the floor. In moments she was surrounded by several ladies clucking their concern—her mother was one of them.

"Oh my, Lucinda, I beg your pardon." Lady Willow bustled near. "I do not understand why the automaton sprang forward when it was securely latched. My deepest apologies."

" 'Tis nothing," Lucinda mumbled, but her eye smarted.

"Here, let me see," Lord Grafton said. "Ladies, if you please, give me room." When the guests backed away, he leaned close. She could smell his spicy cologne. "You must pull your hand away."

She did as bid and dropped her hand away. But it was difficult to open her eye because it stung and watered terribly. If she tried to open it even slightly, she had to quickly close it again.

His arm brushed hers and she felt him lean even closer. "Can you open your eye?" His breath was warm upon her face and she detected a hint of cloves.

"Dougie," Lady Grafton said, "her eye is swelling. You had best get her to the kitchens where Cook can place a cold steak upon it."

"Goodness, a gunshot to your arm and now this," Lucinda's mother said. "Lucinda, you will be black-and-blue from head to toe."

"Gunshot?" Mrs. Lindley asked.

"Mother, please, 'tis nothing," Lucinda interrupted. She did not wish to broadcast what had happened yesterday.

"The Dowager Lady Darrow was accidentally nicked by a poacher's bullet yesterday while we gathered greenery in the field," Lord Grafton explained.

"Never say so, Grafton! Did you let the constable know? Poachers? Goodness, they will be at Ivy Park next." Mrs. Wakeham's voice was shrill.

"We can discuss this later." Lord Grafton stood and extended his hand. "I shall escort the dowager to our cook."

Lucinda took his hand. She wanted out of the drawing room. The ladies were in a dither and the gentlemen tried their best to calm them. Lady Grafton's voice rang above the din as she explained that Mr. Sinclair and her son had seen to the matter and that no one need fear poachers.

When they were in the hall, Lucinda finally asked,

"Why did you tell them?" She held her eye closed with one hand while her other rested in Lord Grafton's grasp.

"Thought it might be good to address your mishap as a run-in with poachers."

"Why?"

"So Robbie and I could see the reactions of our guests."

"And? What did you see?"

"Well, Sir Leonard did not seem fazed, nor did his wife."

"Sir Leonard is drunk, and Lady Darrow does not like me one whit."

"Why do you say that?"

Lucinda shrugged her shoulders. "Just a feeling, I suppose. Perhaps she wishes the bullet had done its job."

"Lucinda," he said with warning tone.

She was already tired of the charade and perhaps a little more shaken by the run-in with the toy than she cared to admit.

"I do not wish to be reminded of what that bullet might have done. Even so, I will definitely take a closer interest in Lady Darrow."

They continued down the hallway and Lucinda felt Lord Grafton's fingers twine with hers. His grip was firm and warm. She held on tightly, trying to wring whatever comfort she could out of the contact. "What of Mr. Lewes? What did he do?"

"He appeared to be genuinely shocked by the news."

She shook her head. " 'Tis like a needle in a hay-stack. What if none of them are responsible?"

"I believe something will turn up soon to give us a clue."

She shivered. She was not sure that boded well for her welfare. They entered the kitchens, which had been cleaned and closed up for the night.

Without warning, Lord Grafton lifted her up and set her upon the table.

She gasped. "You could have warned me."

He laughed softly. "I beg your pardon."

She kept her eyes closed. Her injured eye was tolerable as long as she kept it completely closed. She heard Grafton shuffle and clang about the kitchen. "Perhaps you should send for Cook."

"I know where they keep things," he said.

She opened her good eye. "Do you?"

"Where do you think I go if I wish to sample what is planned for dinner or what is left afterward late at night?"

It was her turn to laugh. A vision of the lofty Lord Grafton scrounging in the kitchen for something to eat was completely at odds with the stiff-necked image he portrayed. Perhaps he was not quite so high in the instep after all.

"Here we are." He offered her a plate with a small red beefsteak. "Place this upon your eye."

She took the raw beef between her fingers, then slapped it over her closed eye. The cold penetrated her skin immediately. She sat still for a few minutes with both eyes closed and listened as Lord Grafton washed his hands and moved about. "It does feels better," she said.

"Good, let's have a look at it, shall we? Can you open it?"

She blinked several times before she could keep her eye open on its own. Her vision was fuzzy, but Lord Grafton's face cleared before her.

He stared into her injured eye, then stepped back and dipped the edge of a towel in a small basin of water. After he squeezed out the excess water, he gently wiped away the effects of the beef. "Can you keep your eye open now?"

Lucinda failed to still her racing heart. She opened both eyes wide as Lord Grafton peered into them. She held her breath as he tipped her chin up, then sideways, in order to look more closely into her injured eye.

"Blink a couple of times."

She did as asked.

"Better?" His voice was soft and dangerously low.

"Much better," she whispered.

"But more time under the steak will help the swelling." He smiled.

She smiled in return.

He stood close. He did not touch her, but his hands were planted upon the table on either side of her and she felt his warmth as dizzyingly as if he had embraced her. He still did not move away from her. Her breath caught when his gaze shifted to her mouth. She dared not move or breathe.

"I am going to kiss you," he murmured.

She closed her eyes and waited, afraid he might change his mind.

Soft as a breeze against her skin, his lips settled upon hers. She leaned into his gentle ministrations and kissed him back, ever so lightly. A warm haze washed over her and she swore the very table spun beneath her. She tried to brace herself from falling backward and her hands gripped Lord Grafton's wrists.

She felt the rapid beat of his pulse. His lips parted and she felt him coaxing her to do the same. Then panic struck.

What should she do?

She could hardly respond the way she wished or he would think her a complete wanton. She did not need a plunging neckline to shame her when her desire would easily take care of that score. She knew what he had started and feared she might be too weak to stop it.

Abruptly, she pulled back. "Grafton, please, they will wonder what takes us so long."

He stared at her, his gaze searching for something. And then he stood and straightened his cravat. "Indeed, you are correct." He offered her his hand to help her off from the table, then quickly let go.

Bereft of his touch and worried by his haughty silence as he gathered up the plate and covered the beefsteak with shaved ice, she blathered on awkwardly, "I think I should retire for the evening and lay the beefsteak upon my eye. It feels like it is swelling again. Yes, I do believe I will retire, but I should tell my mother."

With his head held high, he offered her his arm. "I will send your mother to you."

She laid her hand upon his sleeve, completely at a loss for words. Somehow, she had offended him. Yet he had kissed her! She wondered why.

He looked at her but she could not read his mood or the thoughts behind his decidedly cool gray gaze.

Chapter Eleven

*G*rafton escorted Lucinda to the stairs. What had possessed him to kiss her? He knew very well what—he had stood too close to her. When he had breathed in the intoxicating scent of her floral perfume, his head pounded with desire. It did not help matters when he felt her bosom brush against the outside of his jacket as he checked her eye.

He sighed. "Lucinda, a moment, please."

She stood poised on the bottom stair, waiting.

"I understand what you must be going through, knowing the danger that lurks within these very walls. I assure you that Robbie and I will do everything in our power to keep you safe."

"Of course, I know that you will." She held the plate he had prepared. If he did not let her go, the ice would melt, and the blasted beefsteak would be no good to her warm. But he was loath to let her go just yet. He knew beneath the calm exterior she showed the world, a very frightened young woman resided. He longed to ease that fear, if only with a kiss. But that was hardly the proper way to offer comfort. She had made him embarrassingly aware of that.

He cleared his throat. "This evening . . ." He coughed. "In the kitchen." He pulled at his cravat. What was he trying to do? Apologize? He was not the least bit sorry for kissing her. He wanted to do it again, right here in the hall.

"Lord Grafton, please. Do not give it another thought." She dismissed it with a wave of her hand.

Grafton stared at her.

Her smile was soft and she appeared completely unconcerned. Perhaps she was used to men kissing her unexpectedly. No doubt, she welcomed such advances. Just how many men had she kissed in London hoping to garner an offer from one of them?

His ire rose. He did not kiss just anyone! But he had. He had just kissed a newly widowed woman he had no business trifling with. She was not a green girl even if she was widowed before her wedding night. He need not worry about compromising her, but she could at least *pretend* to be shocked by his behavior—he certainly was.

She stood waiting for him to say something. Her face radiated calm like a serene pool of still water. He envied her control. He felt anything but in control!

"Very well, I shall give your regrets to our guests."

"Thank you, Grafton, and good evening." She turned and started up the stairs.

He watched her until she made it to the top; then he headed for the drawing room. When he entered, Sir Leonard's wife was huddled in a corner with Mrs. Wakeham and Mrs. Lindley. They stopped whispering when they saw him and their cheeks reddened with abashment for being caught gossiping. He knew he had been the topic of their hushed conversation.

"How is Lucinda?" his mother asked.

A chorus of agreement sounded from the other guests.

"She is fine," he said. "She needs to let a cold beefsteak do its job and would rather retire to her room for that. She begs your pardon for not rejoining the party." He turned to Mrs. Bronwell and quietly said, "She would like your help, ma'am."

Mrs. Bronwell rose immediately. "Of course. Good evening. I shall tend to my daughter."

"Yes, of course," Lady Willow murmured. "Give your daughter my deepest apology for her injury. Dratted toy. I shall inquire after her on the morrow."

When Mrs. Bronwell left, the others decided to call it a night. Lady Darrow poked her snoring husband, and the two of them said their good evenings. The rest of the guests retired as well.

After all had gone, Lord Grafton scooped up the toy that had given Lucinda so much trouble and studied it. The carved wooden clown had been made to coil tightly with a latch that could be unhooked in order for the toy to spring.

He practiced coiling, latching, and unlatching it to observe the force with which the toy sprang to life. An interesting choice of gift for an adult. But then the Lindleys had received toys as well, and they intended to give them to their children at home with their governess. Master Thomas would no doubt receive this wooden toy and be glad for it.

"You were gone quite some time." His mother laid her hand upon Grafton's shoulder.

"Had to prepare the beefsteak with chipped ice." He did not dare look at his mother. She would know in an instant what had happened, and browbeat him into confessing and then plague him to make amends by offering for Lucinda's hand. He was certainly turning maudlin, if he feared his own mother! She waited for his answer.

"She may end up with a bit of a rainbow about her eye," he said.

"A black eye would indeed be dreadful." His mother paced the rug, her expression pensive.

When she did not tease him, he knew something was wrong. "What it is, Mother?"

"The ladies were beginning to talk."

Still holding the toy, he ran a hand through his hair. "What did they say?"

"Silly things really—jesting that you might find mistletoe instead of a beefsteak. You did take a rather long time, dear."

Grafton felt his face heat. When he finally looked at his mother, she wore a knowing smile. But he remained silent.

She slumped into a chair. "Dougie, this is all very strange, entertaining people we normally would not. It angers me to think someone wishes to harm Lucinda."

"As it does me." He fiddled with the toy again. Unlatching it, then watching it spring.

"Must you keep playing with that toy?"

He regretted the strain he had placed upon his mother, but knew in the end, he would keep his word of honor to Sir Alaric. "It would appear that the latch was not in place when Lucinda opened the box and peered inside. I simply do not understand why the toy did not leap forth before she had taken off the top. There's quite a bit of force in this little toy."

Her mother let out a sigh. "I do not know, dear. All the gifts were shifted from one person to another so many times; perhaps that jiggled the latch free. I cannot believe Lady Willow meant the box for Lucinda. There was far too much commotion."

Grafton shook his head. It was simply an accident, nothing more. "Of course, you are quite right."

The next morning, Lucinda was glad that her eye, though still a little red, was no worse for wear. The swelling had gone down and only a trace of yellowish bruising could be seen near her nose.

Even so, she was not up to facing Lord Grafton this morning, not after that kiss. Her insides had been in turmoil ever since last night. She could do nothing to share these new feelings for Lord Grafton unless he approached her, which she knew better than to expect.

She ordered a tray and stayed in her room. She hoped she could act normal around him when she saw him again. She ran through any number of things he might say to her and planned her reactions accordingly. When she faced Lord Grafton, she would be prepared.

After she had finished her light repast, a knock at her door produced Lady Grafton. "I hope I am not disturbing you too early," she said.

"I have always been an early riser. Please come in and sit down."

Lady Grafton settled onto the settee near the fire. "I wanted to see for myself that you were fine. Dougie worried that you might have a black eye." She smiled. "I am glad that he was wrong."

"Me too," Lucinda said.

"My son told me about Sir Alaric and your *accidents*." Lady Grafton reached out her hand. "You can come to me if you need to, my dear. About anything." She gave her a pointed look that meant her ears were available for far more than simply the current situation.

Lucinda took her offered hand and squeezed. "Thank you, ma'am." She let go as Lady Grafton rose from the small couch. She quickly said, "Please do not say anything to my mother. Her health is too fragile and she will worry herself sick."

"I understand."

Lucinda took a deep breath. "And I am grateful to your son."

Lady Grafton's eyes brightened with pleasure. "He is honored to protect one so lovely."

Lucinda flushed with warmth. If only she could ask what *he* thought of her. But a son would hardly confess such a thing to his mother. An awkward silence hung between them as if Lady Grafton waited for Lucinda to say something more. But Lucinda could not muster the courage to admit she cared deeply for the noble Lord Grafton.

Lady Grafton gave her an encouraging nod, then asked, "After nuncheon I must deliver the Boxing Day gifts. Would you care to join me? You may bring your sister Bethany too, if she wishes to come." Lady Grafton rose to leave. "It will give you an opportunity to meet our tenants. You missed our open house, and besides, it may do you good to get away from all this for a couple of hours."

"I should like that above all things," Lucinda said. And she meant it.

The cold air bit hard inside her chest when she breathed deeply, but she was glad to quit Arden Hall. Long white fingerlike wisps of smoke curled from cottage chimneys as they made their way from one home to the next. Lord Grafton had decided to stay behind with the guests, but sent Mr. Sinclair in his place to play the role of protector.

Lucinda could not help but be impressed by the solid construction of each home. Lord Grafton clearly took care in ensuring solid shelter for his tenants. Inside the most humble of cottages, the fireplaces were vented properly and the ceilings were dry. There were no pans scattered upon the floor as a telltale sign of leaks.

All day, they were greeted with warmth and cheer. Lord Grafton's tenants expressed their gratitude for the gifts they received in addition to the generous Christmas Eve celebration. Lord Grafton did right by his people.

As they visited the last few houses on foot, Lucinda lagged behind with Mr. Sinclair, who rubbed his mitten-clad hands together.

"A cold morning," he said. "I do believe we might see snow."

"I think you are correct." She kept her hands tucked inside her warm black muff. "Thank you, Mr. Sinclair, for joining us."

"Grafton would have come himself, but he was not inclined to the leave the guests."

"And the hall unprotected," Lucinda added. Perhaps he too did not wish to face her after their awkward parting.

Mr. Sinclair laughed. "Exactly so. You sound as though you know him well."

"Oh no," Lucinda hastened to add. "A guess, merely. Have you known Lord Grafton a long time?"

"We were at Eton together, but we met before that, when my father used to have a home near here."

"Has Lord Grafton always been a serious man?" she asked.

Mr. Sinclair laughed. "Serious. Now there's a polite way of describing him."

Lucinda felt her cheeks heat.

"I think because his sire was so utterly irresponsible, Grafton felt he had to care for his family from an early age. He took over the ledgers and estate management from his father's bailiff when he was barely finished with his studies at Oxford. His sire, glad to be rid of the extra expense, let his son be. As long as his father was kept plump in funds, he did not care who oversaw the details."

She remembered Lord Grafton telling her that his father had not been a good man. Lord Grafton obviously learned what not do from his papa instead of the reverse. It was no wonder that Lady Grafton had such pride in her son.

She spied Bethany waiting for them to catch up while Lady Grafton entered the last house.

"What have the two of you been discussing with

such merry contemplation?" Bethany asked with a twinkle of mischief in her eyes.

Mr. Sinclair chuckled, then said, "My employer of course."

Bethany looked pointedly at Lucinda. "An interesting subject, I am sure."

"Come along, Bethany. Let us see if Lady Grafton needs our aide," Lucinda said.

Later that afternoon, Lucinda sat down next to her mother for tea in the drawing room. The men had gone into the fields to hunt pheasant and to search for poachers in order to assure the ladies that they were gone.

Lucinda's mother pulled out her small hoop of needlepoint. She was monogramming a new set of handkerchiefs for Thomas to take with him when he returned to Eton.

Lady Willow approached with a swish of silk. "My dear Lucinda, how is your eye? I feel terrible about what happened last night."

Lucinda shrugged her shoulders. "Please do not let it trouble you. My eye is just fine."

"Oh, but you have a bruise forming. I left a note for you this morning, but you had already gone with Lady Grafton to deliver Boxing Day gifts."

"I found it when I returned. Thank you, but you need not apologize. Accidents happen."

"What is this I hear?" Lady Darrow had entered the room. "You delivered Boxing Day gifts to the Grafton tenants?" She sat down next to Lady Willow.

Lucinda's mother gazed at the two women, her brow furrowed.

"I did, along with my sister and Mr. Sinclair."

"Much too cold to be out of doors," Lady Darrow sniffed. "A person could catch their death."

Lucinda dropped the ball of thread she had been holding. When she sat back, she noticed the odd light in her mother's eye as she cast a glance from Lady Darrow to Lady Willow.

"Mrs. Bronwell." Lady Willow patted Lucinda's mother's hand. "Do not be troubled. I am certain your daughter suffered no ill effects from the low temperatures."

Lady Darrow went on as if Lady Willow had not spoken. "Your presence with Lady Grafton will no doubt set the village tongues to wagging. Might we inquire if Lord Grafton has found his bride?"

Lady Willow cast Lady Darrow a horrified look. "Lucinda is mourning Sir Alaric."

"Yes, of course, but with a fine specimen like Grafton offering Lucinda his protection . . ." Lady Darrow said.

Lucinda wished she could crawl into a hole and disappear. Lady Darrow made it sound as if she had become Lord Grafton's mistress. Even her mother's brows shot up with shock.

Too late Lady Darrow realized the error of her statement. "That is to say, he is truly protecting her, not offering—well." Her face paled with uneasiness and her fingers nervously plucked at the fringe upon her shawl.

Lady Willow smiled kindly and patted Lucinda's hand. "Of course he is, dear. 'Tis only that the gossips cannot help but wonder about your stay at Arden Hall after the funeral."

Mrs. Lindley had entered in the middle of the conversation. "I have heard titters at church."

"And I." Mrs. Wakeham was not far behind.

Lucinda took pity on Lady Darrow, who looked aghast at her mixed meanings. "After the accident, it was difficult for me to travel," Lucinda said. "I was very ill. After the funeral, with Lady Grafton planning this party, I could not do otherwise but help her as repayment for their kindness after the accident."

"Of course," Lady Willow said. "No sense in traveling nearly to Oxford only to return within a month."

"Exactly so," Lucinda said, but wondered if Lady Willow teased her. She could have easily gone home and returned, but then the roads could be treacherous in December. Fortunately, the housekeeper brought the tea cart and the subject was dropped. "I did not know you knew where I lived."

"I have heard of the Bronwells from Bronley Manor, my dear," said Lady Willow.

"Oh." Lucinda was not surprised. The entire *ton* knew of her lot and where she had come from.

"Perhaps you should pour, Lucinda. Lady Grafton will no doubt join us directly," her mother said.

"Of course." She stood to do as her mother bid.

"Here, let me help you," Lady Willow said.

Sir Leonard's sisters acted slightly offended that Lucinda would take the hostess' place in pouring tea, but thankfully they kept still. Perhaps Lady Willow's intervention allayed their fears that Lucinda was overstepping her bounds. Lady Darrow chattered on endlessly about all they had to do to settle into Ivy Park to anyone who pretended to listen.

When tea had been served, Lady Willow offered the last cup to Lucinda just as Lady Grafton arrived with profuse apologies. She had been tied up with Cook over the evening's menu for dinner. The ladies scattered about the room after tea to enjoy a book by the fire, practice at the pianoforte, or work on embroidery or watercolors.

"Lucinda," her mother whispered.

She leaned closer. "What is it?"

"I remember where I have seen Lady Darrow and Lady Willow before." Her mother's voice dipped even lower. "Your father and I were at a house party and I would swear an oath that Sir Leonard's wife was once Lady Willow's abigail."

Lucinda looked at her mother. "You must have been mistaken."

"I am not. It has only just become clear to me."

Lucinda looked at the two women, grateful that no one had overheard her mother's claim. Could it be true?

Dinner was again held in the great room—the heart of Arden Hall for centuries. Amid the festive swags of greenery, the paper chains, and the crackling of an enormous fire made with the Yule Log, musicians played softly in the corner.

Grafton thought his mother had done it up a bit too brown, as if no one wore mourning clothes. But, then again, it was Christmas—a time of celebration. They could hardly mope about all week or sit and look at one another.

Dinner progressed and the gentlemen chose to forgo their port in order to allow the footmen to clear the table away for dancing. Grafton stood next to the huge hearth when his mother approached him.

"You must lead the dancing, Dougie."

He did not care much for dancing, but when called upon to do his duty, he could muster a graceful leg. "Shall we start it then, Mother?" He offered her his arm.

"No, no, not me. Perhaps you can lead out Lady Willow, for propriety's sake. Mr. Sinclair can partner Miss Bethany. That should at least get things going."

He raised his brow. Of course, since Lady Willow was the highest-ranking lady beside his mother in attendance, he would have to ask her first. Very well, he would do his duty.

He approached Lady Willow just as his mother put a bug into Robbie's ear. His solicitor looked only too cheerful to do as his mother asked and Miss Bethany was certainly willing. But he could not keep watch over them, just now.

"Lady Willow?" He bowed.

She turned away from Mrs. Wakeham. "Lord Grafton."

"Perhaps you will honor me with this dance?" He offered her his hand.

"I would be delighted." She smiled.

Once they formed a line among the four of them, others joined in to make up their sets for a quadrille. He doubted they would dance all night since they were a small party, but nonetheless, the ladies looked eager to join in. He was surprised and a little alarmed to see Mr. Lewes lead a hesitant Lucinda into line. And then the Wakehams joined in and blocked his view.

The music started and they danced the quadrille with no incidents of injury or accident. They moved through several more dances and Lucinda did not lack for partners. Each time Grafton approached, Robbie or Mr. Lindley dragged her off for a dance. Even Sir Leonard had asked for a turn.

When the musicians finally took a break to surround the wassail bowl, Grafton caught a glimpse of Lucinda slipping out the door to the courtyard.

Without calling attention to his departure, he followed her. Once outside, he spied her standing not far off, looking over the fields. A few flakes of snow floated in the cold night air.

"You will catch your death out here," he said, then immediately regretted it when her eyes widened with fear. "I mean, from the cold."

"Lady Darrow said the very same thing earlier today about the cold." Lucinda shook her head as if to clear it from the haunting thought. "I simply needed some fresh air. I promise I shan't be long and I will remain close to the house." Her eyes pleaded with him to let her stay.

He held up his hand. "I did not come out here to ring a peal over you." He moved closer to her. "In fact, I followed you in order to apologize." He held his breath.

Her eyes, normally a bright blue, looked shiny and black in the darkness. "Whatever for?"

"I had no right to kiss you." He thought he saw a hint of disappointment that was quickly controlled into a bland smile.

"You meant no harm and I certainly took no offense."

Exactly so! He did not know why her nonchalance to his romantic overture bothered him so. He wanted something more from her than calm indifference. "You are most gracious." What more could he possibly say?

She turned away and stared out over his land. The snowflakes increased steadily, and stuck to the grass instead of melting. "So pretty," she murmured.

"The snow?"

"See how the flakes flutter and dance in the wind without a care in the world?"

He had never really looked at snowflakes before, but they were indeed beautiful in their simplicity. He watched the snow drop silently upon the ground, where it glistened from the light shining from inside the hall. He thought about what she must be feeling, virtually trapped in his home with a madman bent on doing her harm. "One day you will be carefree again."

She glanced up at him with a lost look in her eyes. "With great wealth comes great responsibility."

Her words surprised him. He had always held the same view, one that was completely at odds with the frivolous nature of society. "Indeed, but there can be pride and joy in the way one handles such responsibility."

"How will I know what is the best way?"

She drew him like a magnet. Against his better judgment, he cupped her chin with his hand and caressed her cheek. "Trust your heart."

Chapter Twelve

Lucinda looked into Lord Grafton's eyes and ached to lean into his warm caress. But how could she? He had just begged her pardon for kissing her! She could hardly attempt another one when it was so very obvious that he regretted his actions.

"I do not think I can trust my heart, Lord Grafton." It was wildly misbehaving at the moment, just from her looking at him. She stepped away from him before she did something she would regret.

"And why is that?" His eyes narrowed, but he revealed nothing.

If the truth were told, she had stopped making decisions with her heart after her father died. Her heart had been broken as she watched her grief-stricken mother sell off heirlooms that had been in the Bronwell family for generations. So she had firmly followed her head and put away all notions of love and happily ever after—until now. Staring into his eyes, she craved those things and realized with alarming clarity that she wanted them with him. "I am quite used to ignoring its existence," she said.

He looked uncomfortable and chaffed his hands. "It is cold out here. I had best go back inside." He hesitated. "Are you coming?"

Disappointment pricked her. She had hoped for a hint of warmer feelings from him—she had left the door wide open for him to step through but he chose to change the subject and leave. "In a moment." Her ignored heart was making its presence known very loudly with a painful little ache of heaviness.

He watched her a moment, his brow furrowed. "Do not stray from the house," he said and turned on his heel.

"Of course not," she whispered. She heard the click of his evening shoes on the flagstone and then he entered the hall with a snap of a closed door behind him. And she was alone with her thoughts. Why must she admire a man who showed no hope of returning her feelings?

A sheltered bench nestled in the curve of an evergreen hedge with a canopy of leafless vines made the perfect hideaway for a few more moments of solitude. She stepped toward it and sat down. The snow had hardly touched the stone seat, but the bitter cold permeated her fine merino gown. She did not care. For now, she wished only to watch the snowflakes fall.

She heard the telltale swish of silk fabric nearby and her spine stiffened. She stood and peeked through the dense hedge. Two people stood outside on the flagstone away from the windows. The woman was Lady Darrow, but she did not recognize the man who was with her. They argued quietly, their whispers strained, but muffled.

Silent as the falling snow, she watched and eventually the two embraced. The man was certainly not Sir Leonard! He was much taller and wore a greatcoat with many capes and a tall hat much like a coachman might wear.

Lucinda breathed slowly, and dread filled her. Was Lady Darrow carrying on an affair with a servant? Her mother's charge that Lady Darrow was once Lady Willow's servant, forgotten till now, blared into her thoughts. Perhaps Lady Darrow and her caped coachman had killed Sir Alaric, and were even now planning Lucinda's doom.

She was too far away to discern their whispers but the tone changed to soothing encouragement. She could hardly move closer without being seen, but she longed to know what they said.

The cold grabbed hold of her with an icy grip and she shivered until she trembled. Rubbing her arms in an attempt to keep warm, she waited until she heard nothing for several minutes before she chanced coming out from the covered alcove.

There was no sign of Lady Darrow or the man she had embraced. Quickly Lucinda ran to the door, opened it, and stepped directly into Lord Grafton's chest.

His arms came up around her, engulfing her in warmth. "You are shaking with cold."

"I must speak to you." Her heart pumped with fear.

He looked around to make sure no one had noticed them. "Come," he said softly. "To my study."

Silently they made their way down the hall. She

stepped past him when he opened the door and quickly made for a chair near the dwindling fire.

Without a word Lord Grafton stoked the glowing coals until they burst into flames and he threw a couple small logs on top. Then he pulled a chair close and sat down directly across from her. With their knees touching, he pulled her hands into his. "Tell me."

She took a deep breath. "I saw Lady Darrow with a gentleman in the courtyard just now. The man was not Sir Leonard and the two of them embraced."

"Did you see the man's face? Is he a guest?"

"He wore a coat and hat much like a coachman's."

"A coachman?"

"That is not all," Lucinda said quickly. "My mother thinks Lady Darrow was once in Lady Willow's employ before her come-out in Bath. I cast the thought away, thinking my mother mistaken, but after seeing her with that coachman—perhaps my mother is correct. What if they are the ones who killed Alaric, and tried to kill me? Somehow they forced Lady Willow into sponsoring her come-out." She felt the panic rising in her throat and clamped her mouth shut.

Lord Grafton's eyes grew wide.

"Did you ever find out where Lady Darrow came from?" Lucinda asked.

"No, but we can start searching Lady Willow's staff of servants for the last few years and see what we find."

"When?" She clung to his hands.

"I shall speak to Robbie tonight. His man of information searched out the staff at Ivy Park and found nothing regarding the cut to your saddle, but perhaps we did not look deep enough."

Lucinda eyes widened. "You sound as if you have done this before."

"Indeed, we have. I had my father followed in order to keep him from blundering into a scandal that my mother would never have been able to live down."

"Goodness."

"Robbie has excellent contacts. He will make a powerful barrister one day soon." He squeezed her hands. "Thank you for coming to me. We will find out to whom this coachman belongs on the morrow. If the snow holds, a sleigh ride might be perfect to draw out the guests' coachmen."

"But I did not see his face."

"There may be other things you remember once you are again in his presence. We must do all that we can." He stood. "Come, we best return. When you did not come back straightaway, I had to find you."

Had he worried about her then? She stood on shaking legs and her courage faltered. She did not want to return to the party.

"Lucinda?"

She closed her eyes and bit down on her lower lip to keep it from trembling. "I am afraid to face her," she whispered. "What if she is the one . . . ?"

Lord Grafton drew her into his arms. "Do not be afraid. She cannot harm you. I won't let her. No one will ever hurt you again, I promise."

She stayed in his arms, drawing strength from his

oath to protect her, believing he would keep her safe. She relaxed in the warmth of his embrace.

"We must return, my dear." His lips brushed her temple and his hands left a trail of heat where he had rubbed her back. "I need you to be strong just a little longer."

She could not turn tail and run like a coward now, not when they were close to finding out the truth. If Lady Darrow was responsible, she wanted to help uncover her part in the deed. "Very well, let us go back to the party."

Later that night, Grafton met with Robbie and relayed everything Lucinda had told him. "We must find out if a Sylvia Harris worked for Lady Willow and when."

Robbie lounged in the chair that Lucinda had sat in earlier in the evening. "Seems too fantastic that Lady Willow would sponsor her servant."

"Mrs. Bronwell might be mistaken or perhaps Lady Willow was coerced somehow. We must at least look into it now that we have something specific to look for."

"Indeed. I have already sent a footman to my man of inquiry."

"Who is the fellow?"

"A friend of sorts."

Grafton nodded. It did not matter who Robbie used as long as they got to the bottom of the mystery. His suspicions had leaned toward Lady Darrow all along but he dared not rule out Mr. Lewes just yet. And what of Lady Willow? Why would she sponsor Sylvia Harris' come-out? It was obvious that Lady

Darrow had been disappointed by Lucinda's portion—she wanted it all.

The next morning Lucinda woke feeling like she had drunk far more wassail than in fact she had. Her head ached and her mouth was dry as dead leaves scattered on the ground. She roused enough strength to get out of bed and padded over to the fire. Thankfully, the grate in her room had been stoked into cozy flames. She had slept so soundly, she had not even heard the maid enter her room.

She opened the heavy curtains that had been closed against the cold glass and smiled despite her throbbing head. The ground was covered with a thick layer of snow. The sun peeked out from behind gray clouds only to disappear again. Darkness hung in the western sky and Lucinda knew they were in for inclement weather.

Despite everything that had happened, a rush of pleasure surged through her. She loved the clean look of fresh snow and the feel of crisp air on her skin. She loved this time of year and heartily looked forward to a sleigh ride, even if it meant coming face-to-face with the mysterious coachman she had seen last night.

Once washed and dressed, she headed downstairs to the breakfast room. Hoping to find Lord Grafton, she swallowed her disappointment when the Wakehams, the Lindleys, and Lady Willow greeted her instead.

"Did you rest well?" Lady Willow asked.

"I slept much later than I expected."

"We all have," Mrs. Lindley said. "I think the wassail bowl was a little strong."

Lucinda smiled, glad that she was not the only one not quite feeling up to snuff. She went to the sideboard and filled her plate with buttered eggs and rashers of bacon as if she was famished. She poured a cup of tea and settled down to eat. In no time she had finished every morsel and the pounding in her head lessened considerably.

"Where are the gentlemen?" she finally asked.

Mrs. Lindley and Mrs. Wakeham exchanged looks as if they knew she was interested in the whereabouts of only one man.

Lady Willow spoke first. "They are checking the thickness of the ice on the pond. If it stays cold, we shall no doubt be skating before the week is out."

"I love to skate," Mrs. Wakeham added. "We brought our skates just in case. One never knows in December."

Lucinda nodded her agreement. Her family had often spent their winters gliding upon their little pond at Bronley Manor, but usually not before January.

"Lucinda, dear," Lady Willow said, "might you and your mother visit with me this afternoon? I have a very delicate needlepoint and I am simply at a loss for what to do next. I noticed that your mother is a marvel with her needle and thread."

"We will be honored to help," Lucinda said. Perhaps she might find out more about her relationship with Lady Darrow.

"Good day, everyone." Lady Darrow entered with a swish of silk fabric.

The very sound made Lucinda's blood freeze. She looked up from her plate to spy Sir Leonard tagging along behind his wife, and she felt sorry for him. Alaric's nephew had been manipulated into marriage, she would wager. But if the truth were told, he did not look too sorry for it.

Lady Darrow did not have the rough speech of a servant, but then many upper servants aped their betters in manners. And she may have come from a genteel upbringing.

Lucinda watched her as closely as possible, but her presence was too unnerving. She stood. "If you will excuse me, I think I shall fetch a warmer wrap."

The guests nodded, unconcerned.

Lucinda left the breakfast room and met Lord Grafton in the hall.

"Lucinda," he said softly, "a word, please." His nose was red from the cold and his dark hair was endearingly blown by the wind.

"Of course."

"Perhaps you might accompany me to the stables this afternoon." His voice dipped to just above the whisper. "See if any of the coachmen look familiar."

"This afternoon I promised to sit with Lady Willow."

His brow furrowed with concern. "Not alone. I do not trust any one of our guests."

"My mother accompanies me."

"Good. Let us grab our coats then."

"I should like to change into warmer boots. It will only take a moment."

He smiled and nodded. "Meet me in my study when you are ready."

In less than a quarter of an hour, she followed Lord Grafton across the snowy ground. He explained that Mr. Lewes' coachman remained at Arden Hall since he did not plan to stay through Twelfth Night. The Darrows had come with the Lindleys and their coachman had been given leave to return home for the holiday. The Wakehams' coachman remained because Mrs. Wakeham did not wish to be without their own transportation should something arise requiring that they leave immediately.

"How is the ice on the lake?" Lucinda asked as they crossed the gravel drive.

"Not yet quite thick enough near the shore, but it should be solid in a couple days. Do you like to skate?"

"Adore it. In fact, I love the snow."

He shook his head and gave her a look as if she were a complete pea goose. "Far too cold for me."

"The dreary cold rain is what I cannot abide. One cannot stay warm when it is so damp."

"I suppose you are correct. You will no doubt appreciate the sleigh ride."

She felt a childish thrill flow through her. When had she last been on a sleigh? "Yes, I will."

"Then we will pull the old thing out and give it a go."

"Thomas will love it," she said.

"How is the lad?"

She knew Lord Grafton had visited her brother the day before. "I spoke with him this morning. He is a tad bored."

"That is to be expected," he said. "I shall stop up to the nursery this afternoon."

"Thomas said he enjoyed your visit yesterday. I thank you for checking on him and Margaret." His kindness touched her deeply.

"No matter, just making sure Lady Anne had everything she needed." He shrugged off her thanks as if uncomfortable with her gratitude.

But she knew he cared, and that warmed her heart more than any Yule log fire. She glanced up at him and her foot slipped on some ice. Lord Grafton steadied her in an instant by draping his arm around her and she melted into him.

"Would not want you to fall," he whispered close to her ear, sending a delicious shiver down her spine. He kept his arm about her until they reached the stables.

Before they entered, he leaned even closer. "Have a care to look at each man," he said softly. "You might recognize one of them as the fellow embracing Lady Darrow."

The pleasant reprieve from danger was over. They had not come our here for pleasure, nor did Lord Grafton simply wish her company. She had a job to do.

He gave her shoulder an encouraging squeeze.

She looked into his gray gaze. "I will do my best."

"Of course you will." Lord Grafton's expression turned serious. His mouth formed a firm line of resolve.

They entered the warm stables and Lucinda inhaled the comforting smells of horse and hay. The stable was indeed full and lively. Horses munched their oats and stable boys whistled while cleaning stalls. Grooms bustled about attending to their daily chores.

She followed Lord Grafton toward the back, where some of the men lounged near the fireplace while others rubbed the leather saddles down with oil. Everyone stopped when they realized Lord Grafton had entered with a lady.

"Good day, my lord." One of the men pulled at the front of his hair.

"Relax, men," Lord Grafton said. "I wish to show the Dowager Lady Darrow our sleigh. I believe we might actually use it this year."

They walked through the room and Lucinda plastered a smile upon her face as she studied every man. She bid many a happy new year and appeared as cheerfully kind as she could instead of curiously nosy. None of the men looked the least bit familiar, or concerned.

Lord Grafton cocked an eyebrow high, questioning her.

She shook her head. "Nothing, I am afraid."

"Then let us look at the sleigh."

Lucinda smiled when she saw it. The sleigh could easily fit several people at a time. She ran her hand over the leather tethers that were adorned with bells. Looking up at him she said, "It is perfect."

Grafton could not look away from her wide blue eyes or the wisps of blond hair that had escaped from her fur-lined bonnet to tease her rosy cheeks. The thought struck him that it was *she* who was perfect.

"Perhaps Bethany and I might make festive bows for the horses' manes and tails."

"That would be nice," he murmured. He did not care what she did as long as she did it here. The sudden realization that he did not want her to leave Arden Hall washed over him. He was shocked at the strength of his feelings, but they felt right once he accepted them as true.

He enjoyed seeing her face across from him each morning in the breakfast room. He appreciated the joy she took in simple tasks like decorating the hall and now the sleigh. Even though danger lurked, she could still smile and be merry. And he genuinely liked her family.

Perhaps his mother was correct thinking Lucinda might make him a good match. But she faced eleven months of mourning ahead of her. To approach her with sentiments such as these at such an inopportune time just wasn't done. Above all things, he was a respectable man who abided by the rules of good society. He would simply have to wait.

Chapter Thirteen

*T*wo days passed in the grip of a snowstorm, trapping the party indoors. They managed well enough with games of charades and whist or reading in the drawing room until tea was served. Lucinda and her mother sat with Lady Willow each afternoon, to work on embroidery and needlepoint. Each afternoon, however, Lady Darrow sent her regrets, preferring an afternoon nap. She never joined them until dinner.

Lucinda had often caught Lord Grafton deep in thought during their afternoons in the drawing room. She knew his patience ran thin. It did not help matters that they had not yet heard from Robbie's man of inquiry. And Mr. Lewes paced the drawing room floor like a caged animal. He had wished to leave but could not due to the inclement weather.

But today promised to be fine. The morning clouds had dissipated to reveal a brightly shining sun. Everyone, especially Thomas and Margaret, looked forward to an afternoon spent out of doors. The sleigh had been polished and made ready. And the pond proved to be solid, so skating would be available too.

Lucinda hoped she would feel well enough to go. Every morning she stayed abed with a throbbing headache that resulted in casting up her accounts in her chamber pot if she rose too quickly. By midday, after a luncheon tray in her room, she usually felt more the thing and was well enough to join the ladies in the drawing room.

But the previous evening, her head had pounded so hard that she had to forgo joining the others for dinner and retire early. Today, she very much wanted to get out of the house for fresh air. The snows had stopped and she longed to go outside.

Lady Grafton had given her ginger dissolved in hot water and Dr. Warren's pills, which helped to stay her nausea, but her mother was very concerned and wanted to send for a doctor as soon as the roads were passable.

Lucinda assured her mother that merely the stresses of the party and Sir Alaric's death had finally taken hold of her. She did not run a fever and felt tolerably well, with the exception of the headaches, which crashed over her with waves of acute pain. After nearly three days of feeling like a war had been waged inside her head, she would not refuse a visit from Lord Grafton's physician. But she doubted it was anything serious and thought that perhaps the terrible weather had brought it all on.

Lord Grafton tried to hide his concern, but she sensed in him a tightly coiled tension he kept firmly under control. Perhaps his mood would lighten once they were on the sleigh ride. She dearly hoped so.

After a hearty luncheon, Lucinda changed into her warmest wool gown along with thick woolen stockings and half boots. Feeling nearly normal, she was determined to join the others out of doors. She finished lacing her boots when her mother and Bethany stepped into her bedchamber.

"Are you quite certain you are well enough, dear?" Lucinda's mother asked.

"I am. Not a trace of a headache. I feel fine."

Her mother touched her forehead. "Still no fever."

"The fresh air will do me good, Mother."

"I hope so. You have always been such a healthy girl, it distresses me to see you feeling poorly."

Lucinda stood up to bestow a kiss upon her mother's cheek. "I know, dearest. But like I said, I feel fine today. Perhaps the storm aggravated or caused my condition. Now that the sun is shining, I feel whole."

"Promise me you will not overexert yourself."

"I will keep careful watch over her," Bethany, fully dressed for the out of doors, offered with a smile.

Grafton waited for the guests to join him outside for a sleigh ride to the pond. Early this morning, he had checked the ice and it was solid. Not knowing how long the cold weather might last, he intended to make it as enjoyable as possible, especially for Lucinda, who had been plagued with headaches the last couple of days.

With the help of his servants, they cleared off the pond for skating and then built a warming tent. It closed on three sides and had a floor made by throwing a heavy bit of canvas over the snow followed by a thick carpet. Pillows were scattered about along with baskets of food. A large fire raged just outside of the tent, and a heavy iron cauldron filled with mulled wine kept warm over the flames.

Restless, Grafton tapped his foot against the sleigh's runners, knocking off bits of snow and ice. He had this terrible feeling that something was about to happen, but he could not put his finger upon it. He had been waiting for information from Robbie's man, and the longer he went without hearing a word, the more inclined he was to believe that something crucial had been found regarding the identity of the killer.

"I say, Grafton, are you our driver, what?" Sir Leonard bustled down the steps with his wife swaddled in furs by his side.

"What a noble coachman you make," Lady Darrow said.

He cringed, knowing Lucinda had spied the lady's assignation with her coachman a few nights ago. He knew Lady Darrow was the key to the entire mystery, but how to unlock her secrets was yet to be discovered. He could not approach her until he had some sort of proof.

The Wakehams and Lindleys followed with Master Thomas and his keeper, Lady Anne.

"Good day, Master Thomas," Grafton said as he helped the lad into the sleigh.

"Is it true that we may play out of doors all day?"

Grafton winked at him. "As long as your mother approves, yes."

Lady Anne, his mother's friend and a spinster,

clucked her tongue. "But, if you get chilled, you must return to the hall straightaway."

Grafton nearly laughed aloud. The air, though crisp, was softened by brilliant sunshine. It did not feel nearly as cold as the previous two days. If these children were anything like he had been at their age, they would last for hours and be wet to the skin before admitting the need to go back inside.

The sleigh was full and he was about to climb up into the driver's seat when the rest of the Bronwell family emerged from the hall.

He was comforted to see a smiling Lucinda looking the very picture of health. "A beautiful day," he said, knowing she would agree.

"It is. Your sleigh is full. We shall wait for your return."

"Good day, Lucinda." Lady Darrow waved. "So glad to see you up and about."

"Thank you. I am feeling much more the thing."

Grafton snapped the reigns. His horses pulled away and pranced their way through the snow; the jingle of the harness and tethers adorned with bells lifted his spirits despite his suspicions and feeling of foreboding.

But Lady Darrow appeared in earnest with her good wishes toward Lucinda. In fact, he would go so far as to say the woman looked relieved. He shook his head. Regardless of his worries, it would be hard to simply enjoy this day while he waited for word from Robbie's man.

Lucinda watched the sleigh pull away. Lord Grafton's matched bays were incredible specimens of horseflesh. They held their heads proudly and swished their tails as if they too knew it was a festive season.

"I cannot wait to twirl about the ice," Bethany said. "I am glad I brought our skates."

"Very intuitive of you, dearest," Lucinda said. "Where is Margaret?"

"She is coming with Lady Grafton. I believe they are in search of more skates," her mother informed them.

Lord Grafton returned after he had dropped off his first load at the pond's edge. Lucinda and the rest of her family piled in and nestled underneath the heavy rugs.

"Once everyone has been dropped off by the pond, the sleigh rides will start from there for whomever wishes to go," Lord Grafton said.

"You will drive?" Lucinda asked, hoping to sit next to him.

"Of course. I am not skilled upon the ice." He smiled.

"We would not let you fall, would we, Lucy?" Bethany climbed into the front seat and sat next to Lord Grafton, before Lucinda had the chance.

Even so, Lucinda had the pleasure of seeing Lord Grafton's cheeks color. "No," she said softly, "we would not let his lordship fall."

"Ladies," he said, "you needn't 'my lord' me. Please call me Grafton."

They agreed. Bethany turned around, gave their mother a pointed look, and then grinned at Lucinda.

"Do stop," Lucinda whispered a scold.

Bethany mouthed the words, *"I think he likes you."*

Lucinda rolled her eyes. Her sister was definitely no help and too obvious by half.

"Here we are, everyone out," Lord Grafton said.

Lucinda's stomach flipped over as she took Lord Grafton's hand to step out of the sleigh, but she quickly took herself to task. There was no reason to expect anything from Lord Grafton in the way of courtship. Not when she was in mourning, at least. He would never presume to interfere with that.

Besides, he had given her no indication that he wished to call upon her afterward. There was only that one kiss between them. And as ground-shaking as the kiss had been, for her at least, it was hardly worth pinning her hopes upon.

After every willing guest had been delivered to the pond just beyond the hall, Lord Grafton offered to take those who wished to go for a sleigh ride. Lucinda was the first to stand in line, hoping this time to sit next to Lord Grafton. Bethany remained behind to wait for Mr. Sinclair, who had yet to join the party at the pond.

As they huddled together to wait for more riders, Mr. Sinclair appeared on foot wearing a very serious frown that bespoke bad news. He took Lord Grafton aside and the two spoke too low to hear. But Lord Grafton's gaze sought Lucinda's. They had found something, she was sure.

"Forgive me," Lord Grafton said to the guests waiting for a sleigh ride. "I have important business to attend to for the moment. I will send my groom to drive the sleigh."

Lucinda quickly walked toward him, away from the others. "Grafton?"

He waited for her.

"What news?" she asked.

"Robbie's man is waiting in my study. Do take care to remain close to your family until I return."

Lucinda felt a tremor pass through her. Perhaps they might finally solve the mystery and she need not worry any longer that someone might harm her. "Of course."

When Grafton entered his study, a wiry man of medium height stood and bowed.

"This is Mr. Dawson," Robbie said.

Grafton extended his hand. "Let us get straight to the matter, shall we? What have you learned?"

"Something very interesting." Dawson's voice was low and cultured with a slightly foreign accent, as if he had lived abroad.

Grafton glanced quickly at Robbie. What else did his solicitor do on his own time?

Red-faced, Robbie admitted, "We have done some work for Whitehall."

That meant Mr. Dawson was experienced and would no doubt produce trustworthy results. Grafton leaned forward, ready to listen with every fiber of his being.

"Lady Darrow was born Sylvia Harris to genteel shopkeepers who died in a fire at their establishment. Having nowhere to go, Miss Harris went to work for Sir Reginald Teasedale, the same man who had employed her elder brother as second coachman."

"An awful man," Robbie whispered.

Grafton gave him a silencing look.

Robbie shrugged his shoulders. "Go on, then."

Dawson cleared his throat. "Miss Harris worked as a companion for Sir Reginald's wife. Her brother's skill at the ribbons rivaled that of any member of the Four-in-Hand Club. Lord Willow lost to the fellow in a carriage race and offered Mr. Harris a position at much higher wages to become his head coachman."

"How long ago was this?" Grafton asked.

"John Harris went to work for Lord Willow nearly four years ago and remained there until after Lord Willow went into a decline and died thereafter in a carriage accident."

Grafton's eyebrows shot up. "Was Harris the driver?"

"Yes," Dawson replied.

"What of Miss Harris?"

"There is no record of a Miss Harris in Lady Willow's employ, but the servants did state that a young woman named Sylvia came to live with Lady Willow shortly before Lord Willow's death."

Grafton swallowed hard. "Where is John Harris now?" His heart pounded in his ears, but he feared he knew the answer.

"In Sir Leonard Darrow's·employ. Started shortly after Miss Harris married."

"And the coachman for Sir Alaric and Lucinda on their wedding day, I'd wager." Grafton shot to his feet. "I must have a conversation with this John Harris, do you not think?"

Robbie also stood. "I'll go with you."

"No," Grafton said. "Stay here and keep an eye on Lady Darrow. Make certain she goes nowhere near

Lucinda until we know what this scheme of hers and her brother's is about. Mr. Dawson, if you would be so kind as to accompany me?"

Dawson agreed.

Grafton raced to the stables, where he had his horse and one for Mr. Dawson made ready. He scanned the merry scene at the pond and then spotted the sleigh in the distance with Lucinda, her mother, her brother, and the Lindleys aboard. She was safe and sound for now. Robbie would watch over her until he returned.

Vaulting into the saddle, he urged Horatio into a gallop toward Ivy Park.

Chapter Fourteen

Lucinda returned from her sleigh ride to find Mr. Sinclair skating with Bethany. Lord Grafton had not yet returned. She chewed her bottom lip, wondering what they had found.

She cast a nervous glance toward Lady Darrow. The woman stood near the fire with a mug of mulled wine in her hands and an empty look in her eyes. She suddenly turned and her eerie gaze locked with Lucinda's. Lucinda quickly looked away and scurried to join Mr. Sinclair and Bethany upon the ice.

After skating a long while on the pond and drinking a mug of hot wine, Lucinda was ready to return to the main house and take a nap. She had rushed her recovery and now paid the price with a weariness that sank deeper to the bone than even the cold.

"My dear Lucinda, you look positively frozen, come to the fire and warm yourself." Lady Willow linked her arm around Lucinda's.

Lucinda was suddenly so exhausted, she could not think clearly. "Actually, I should like to return to the hall."

"Another headache?" She clucked her tongue. "You have done far too much today. I will walk you back. 'Tis not far and the sleigh is occupied with riders. Come, we can tell your mother and she may walk with us if she wishes. Once at the hall, I shall ring for hot tea."

"That would be very nice." It sounded heavenly. Lucinda looked for her mother and spotted her skating on the ice with Thomas and Margaret circling around her. They were a merry group. Her mother's laughter made her look young and carefree and Lucinda did not have the heart to pull her away.

Bethany and Mr. Sinclair skated together clear across the pond. Lucinda stopped Mrs. Lindley, who looked ready to return to the ice. "Please tell my mother that I have gone back to the hall with Lady Willow."

"You do not look well." Mrs. Lindley's expression was one of genuine concern.

"I am merely tired."

"Very well, I will tell her."

"Come, my dear," Lady Willow said. "We will have you warmed and resting in no time."

Lucinda held on to Lady Willow's arm as they trudged up the small hill toward Arden Hall. It was not very far and Lucinda knew her mother would join her momentarily.

"Have you enjoyed your holiday?" Lady Willow asked.

"I have."

"And so pleasing to have snow, would you not say?"

"A nice diversion from remaining indoors," Lucinda said, then yawned. "I beg your pardon."

Lady Willow patted her hand. "Do not worry. I have just the thing for you."

Lucinda sighed and kept walking. Her feet were cold but she knew she would be warm before a fire with a strong cup of tea in no time.

When they finally entered the hall, their footsteps echoed on the marble.

"Where is Naughton?" Lucinda asked.

"I saw some of the servants enjoying the outdoors. Did you not see them on the ice? I would wager Naughton is there too. Lord Grafton is a generous employer."

Lucinda nodded, although she could not imagine the stuffy butler enjoying a good skate.

"Here, let me take your pelisse. It is quite soaked."

Lucinda did as she was bid.

"Now let us go to the great hall, where the Yule log still burns brightly. I will order tea."

Grafton and Mr. Dawson reigned in their horses outside the stables of Ivy Park. Grafton was off his stallion and striding through the stable door before Mr. Dawson had dismounted.

The main groom pulled his forelock. "My lord?"

"I need to speak with your coachman. Man's name is John Harris."

"Tack room." The groom jerked his head sideways.

Grafton followed the corridor leading to the tack room. Mr. Dawson had caught up and they entered together. A tall man with thick brown hair bent over a table spread with leather reins that he polished with oil. "Are you John Harris?"

The man looked up in surprise. "Who's asking?"

"My name is Arden, Earl of Grafton, and this is Mr. Dawson."

The man recognized Mr. Dawson, but he did not cower. He stood straighter, looking belligerent. "What do you want?"

"Are you John Harris?" Grafton rolled his hands into fists but kept them at his side.

"I am."

"Perhaps you might explain why Sir Alaric Darrow's widow left here with a cut saddle girth."

Harris glanced at Mr. Dawson.

Grafton lunged forward and grabbed Harris by the shirt collar and pinned him against the wall. "I already know Sir Leonard's wife is your sister. Was it she who planned Sir Alaric's death? Did she put you up to threatening his widow?"

Fear flashed in Harris' eyes. He clawed at Grafton's hands. "Please."

"I have enough information to haul you into the magistrate's court. Whether you are guilty or not, it would be enough for them to clap you in irons."

"For the love of God, hear me out," Harris choked.

Grafton let go of the man's shirt. "Then talk."

Harris sank into a chair and ran a shaking hand through his wiry hair. "It is not Sylvia's fault. She is guilty of nothing more than being a pawn in a madwoman's game of revenge—a game that I was too far mired in to keep Sylvia out of."

Grafton felt the hairs on his neck stand on end. "Who is this woman?"

"Lady Willow."

Grafton felt the blood rush from his head. Good God, he had never considered Lady Willow. He had failed to protect Lucinda by telling Robbie to watch the wrong woman!

"We have to get back," he muttered. He did not trust the coachman not to run off if they went by horseback, yet the roads were not clear enough for a carriage. "John Harris, does Ivy Park have a sleigh?"

"It does."

"Then ready it. You can tell me the whole story on our way back to Arden Hall."

"Aye."

Grafton turned to Robbie's man. "Dawson, can you drive?"

"Of course, sir." The fellow looked insulted.

They stayed close to John Harris as he worked. After leaving their horses in the groom's care they pulled away from Ivy Park.

Lucinda followed Lady Willow into the hall and sat down in a chair she pulled close to the hearth. She stretched out her booted feet toward the fire. She would wait to take them off until her mother joined her and they could retire to her room. She should go there this moment, but she did not wish to be rude and she very much desired a cup of tea.

In moments, Mrs. Smith arrived with the tea cart. Lady Willow dismissed the housekeeper and went about the business of pouring.

"There now," Lady Willow said softly. "A perfect dish of tea."

Lucinda turned toward Lady Willow, expecting to

reach for her cup, but a flash of silver caught her attention. Lucinda watched in horror as Lady Willow slid a silver flask back into the folds of her skirt pocket. It was identical to the ones she and Alaric had drunk from on their wedding day. Frightened, she quickly stood.

"What is it dear?" Lady Willow's smile suddenly looked sinister.

"You did it," she whispered.

"Did what, pray?"

"You poisoned Alaric."

Lady Willow continued to walk toward her, teacup in hand. "He had to die," she said calmly.

"Why?" Lucinda scurried behind the chair.

"I loved him too much not to have him." It made no sense and yet she spoke the words as if she spoke of the weather. "He loved you, dear, thought you were the sweetest thing he had ever met. And that is why you too must die."

"No!" Lucinda pushed the chair forward into Lady Willow's path and ran. The heavy wood doors to the huge room were closed. She pushed against them with all her might, but they did not budge.

" 'Tis locked." Lady Willow dangled the keys from her fingers. "So easy to steal from Mrs. Smith since they hung from her waist as if she were a medieval chatelaine."

Lucinda closed her eyes.

"Scream if you like, but I doubt she will hear you. She is long gone. Besides, this is the oldest part of Arden Hall and the walls are thick with stone."

"Mrs. Smith," Lucinda yelled at the top of her lungs, "help me!"

Lady Willow walked closer.

Lucinda knocked over a table and rolled it at her, but the woman was undeterred.

She came closer, slowly sidestepping the table. "There is nowhere to run, Lucinda."

"Please," Lucinda begged. She felt light-headed and weak.

"You are feeling the effects of the arsenic now. I splashed a little in your mulled wine. In fact, I have been pouring tiny amounts in your tea since I arrived. Poor dear, you have been so ill, it will come as no surprise when you take a turn for the worse. The doctor will never know. No one will know."

"Grafton will know," Lucinda said. "He knows that Alaric died from arsenic poisoning."

"Does it really matter? When you are dead, my work is finished." Lady Willow lunged at her.

Lucinda moved away, but Lady Willow was surprisingly fast and strong. She grabbed Lucinda's hair and jerked back hard, causing Lucinda to fall to her knees as blinding pain ripped through her head.

"Come now, Lucinda, you are cold and this brandy will warm you." Lady Willow's face looked as hard as the ice of the pond. Fine lines were visible on her white skin.

Lucinda choked out. "You are mad!"

"Madness is not far from love, my dear." Lady Willow pulled her head back farther, causing Lucinda to cry out. "And I have been lovesick for years. I poisoned my husband for Alaric, but the dratted man had given his word to Willow that he would leave me alone. Alaric was nothing if not a man of his word!"

Lucinda choked on a sob. Her hands flailed to break free, but Lady Willow only wrenched her head back farther each time she moved.

"Now, then, you will drink this." Lady Willow shoved the opened flask into her mouth.

Lucinda kept her throat closed and despite the sharp pain, she dared not cry out or even breathe. The poisoned brandy spilled out of her mouth, pouring down her chin onto her clothes.

"Drink it!"

Lucinda had to do something. With all her might, she turned and swung her arms against Lady Willow's knees.

Lady Willow let go of her hold on Lucinda's hair and fell down with a moan of agony. It was enough time for Lucinda to spit out the remaining brandy and leap to her feet. She searched for a way out. There was only the one door, but the walls were lined with windows.

Her fingers grasped the bottom of a window and she groaned with frustration when it would not open. She went to the next one and it flew open easily. Without a moment's hesitation, she climbed out just as Lady Willow bore down upon her. Her feet hit the snow and she was thankful the great room was on the ground floor.

Lucinda ran, but Lady Willow was out of the window and running behind her. Lucinda's hair was completely undone, and when she looked back, it flew across her face, momentarily blinding her. She slipped in the snow, but righted herself, and that small movement cost her.

Lady Willow grabbed the fabric of her skirt, making her trip and fall into the snow with a grunt.

"Let go of me!"

Lady Willow only laughed wickedly and sat upon her back. With cold, clawlike fingers, she forced Lucinda's face into the snow. Deeper and deeper, Lady Willow pushed her head into the snow-covered ground until Lucinda could not catch her breath. The snow melted into hard, crusty ice that tore at her skin and the bitter cold burned her face. She choked.

Fear like she had never known ripped through her, numbing her. She could hardly move. Her limbs felt heavy and awkward. Lucinda doubted the servants could see her since they were outside the locked great room and unable to see the pond.

Lucinda swiped her bare fingers across the snow in search of anything she might use against her insane attacker. The sound of Lady Willow's wild ranting faded in Lucinda's ears and stars zoomed in from the corners of her eyes. She knew that if she did not do something fast, she would lose consciousness and then she was as good as dead.

An image of Lord Grafton leaning over her when she fell from Ariel flashed through her mind. His eyes had been filled with concern and fear and something else. He would never forgive himself if she let Lady Willow kill her and break his promise.

She had to live.

With a burst of renewed strength, Lucinda pushed against Lady Willow, but she failed to dislodge the heavier woman. Then Lucinda's fingers bumped into the silver flask, lying deep in Lady Willow's pocket.

She fished through the folds of fabric until she grabbed hold of it and felt its weight—no doubt made of real silver.

Her lungs burned in agony as she tried to breath in air and failed. Lucinda quickly swung the flask back hard and connected with Lady Willow's elbow. Lucinda heard a crack, then a howl of pain. It was enough to knock Lady Willow backward.

Lucinda scrambled to her feet and ran away from the back of Arden Hall. Exhausted and out of breath, she leaned against a huge stone fountain in the middle of a side garden. She looked up in time to see Lady Willow coming toward her with a stick, ready to strike.

Lucinda met Lady Willow's blow with her arms raised, her forearms taking the brunt of the impact. White-hot anger and the will to survive took over. Lucinda grabbed hold of Lady Willow's arms and yanked hard. "That is enough out of you," she snarled.

Lucinda launched Lady Willow, sending her falling headlong into the bottom of the empty fountain. Dragging gulp after gulp of cold air into her already sore chest, she ran.

Without looking back to see if Lady Willow was hurt, Lucinda headed toward the pond.

Grafton was stunned after hearing the whole story from John Harris. He had left Lucinda to the machinations of a horrid woman who was quite possibly mad. If anything had happened to her while he was gone, he would never forgive himself. He should have seen it. How could he not have considered the possibility? But it made no sense that a gentlewoman could be that evil.

The Darrows' sleigh was lighter and newer than the one at Arden Hall. It moved easily through the snow and they made quick work of the five miles separating the estates. Pulling into the long drive at Arden Hall, Grafton scanned the pond, where everyone still appeared to be enjoying the activities. His sleigh sat parked next to the warming tent.

"Pull up to the tent," Grafton said.

Mr. Dawson did as bid, but Grafton was impatient to see Lucinda. He hopped out of the sleigh before they had come to a full stop. "Keep an eye on Harris," he said over his shoulder as he ran toward Robbie.

"Grafton." Robbie spread wide his arms. Miss Bethany stood next to him.

"Where is Lucinda? Where is she?" Grafton's gaze searched the party, but she was nowhere in sight.

"Just went up to the house with Lady Willow." Robbie looked at Miss Bethany. "Not twenty minutes ago. We are on our way to join her."

"Good God."

"What is it?" Robbie became serious in an instant.

"Lady Willow is our killer. Lady Darrow and her brother, the coachman, are only accomplices."

Miss Bethany let out a squeal. "Mama," she screamed, "Lucinda is in danger!"

Grafton did not wait to explain the situation. He darted toward the hall. As he ran through the snow, his heart pounded so hard he thought it would break out of his chest. Twenty minutes! Anything could happen in twenty minutes.

Chapter Fifteen

Grafton spotted Lucinda in the distance and his knees weakened with relief. She ran toward him, her gold hair flowing down past her shoulders. Her face was pale except for the redness of her nose and cheeks. She wore no coat and her skirt was torn. She looked like she had been through hell.

She crumpled before she reached him. "Grafton."

"Lucinda!" He ran to her, fell to his knees, and scooped her into his arms. "Dear God, are you all right?" He searched her face and neck for injuries.

Tears streamed down her face and she nearly swooned. "It was Lady Willow." She trembled and shook. "I knocked her into the empty fountain."

He held her tightly. "Please forgive me for not protecting you from her. I should have known she was dangerous."

"You could not have known. She acted so kind, she fooled us all." Her breath was warm against his neck, but her lips and nose were ice-cold.

He picked her up and carried her. "You are frozen."

She dropped her head onto his shoulder with a sigh, but said nothing more.

He looked to the sky and thanked God she was safe. He shuddered with gratitude and something else he could not put to words just now.

Robbie came up behind them. "How is she?"

"Nearly frozen. I need to get her inside. Check the garden fountain for Lady Willow," he said. "Do not let her get away."

Robbie made fast tracks past them. Grafton knew he would take care of the witch. All that mattered was the lady in his arms.

He heard the rest of the guests making their way toward them with groans of dismay and shrieks of fear. He ignored them all. He carried Lucinda as quickly as he could through the snow toward the house. He had to get her out of the cold.

"Naughton!" he bellowed as he entered the hall.

"Sir?" His butler came running with a look of pure anguish.

"Have someone make up the fire in Lucinda's room. Send a footman for the constable and the doctor." The worry in his butler's eyes gave him pause. "She will be fine, Naughton, truly. Please hurry."

"Right away, sir."

Grafton carried a very quiet Lucinda into the nearest room, his study. He stooped to settle her into a chair, but she clung to him, her hands locked behind his neck. "Let go, my love. You are safe now."

"But Lady Willow," she murmured.

"Robbie has gone after her. She cannot cause any more grief." He tore off his coat and wrapped it around her. He rubbed her arms and chaffed her hands, hoping to warm her until her mother arrived.

Her eyes welled up with tears. "I was so afraid. She is quite mad. She poisoned Alaric. She even poisoned her own husband." Her voice caught and broke. "And she tried to do the same to me. She forced that awful brandy on me, but I did not drink it. I spit it out."

"Good girl." He knelt down at her feet and cradled her face between his hands. He searched her eyes, hoping she was truly sound. She had been through an awful shock, a horrifying experience worse than any nightmare.

"I will be right as rain in no time," she whispered with a ghost of a smile tugging at her quivering lips.

It was then that he knew his heart was hers forever. He loved this brave girl, who had thrown convention to the wind in order to secure her family's future. She had more strength of character than anyone he had ever met. He owed her more than mere respect and admiration. He owed her his life and love, if she would accept his arrogant carcass.

The door opened.

"Dougie, how is she?" his mother asked.

He stood, but before he could answer, Mrs. Bronwell bustled forward, pushing him out of the way. "Lucy, dearest, what happened?" She knelt down and took her daughter's hand.

"I am so sorry, Mama," Lucinda said. "I did not want to worry you. Lady Willow poisoned Alaric on our wedding day and tried to do the same to me."

Her mother looked suitably shocked and glanced at Grafton for answers.

He felt the weight of shame upon his shoulders. "I must humbly beg your pardon, Mrs. Bronwell, for keeping you in the dark. It is rather a long story, but the constable has been sent for and we shall get to the bottom of things. The most important priority right now is Lucinda's health. The doctor will be here shortly, but your daughter is chilled to the bone."

"And could use some tea," his mother said quickly.

Lucinda groaned. "Please, no tea."

"Indeed," Grafton said, wondering why she should refuse. He would no doubt find out later. "I must see to Robbie and the others." He glanced at Lucinda.

She gave him an encouraging nod with the hint of a smile and his heart broke.

Without a word, he followed his mother out, leaving his love in the capable hands of Mrs. Bronwell. He had so much to tell Lucinda, but now was not the time. He had responsibilities demanding his attention and she needed to recover from this ordeal.

Stripped out of her wet gown and changed into a dry chemise, Lucinda was helped into bed by her mother. A tray arrived with warm posset and the steaming brew did wonders to warm her insides, but she could not stop shaking. The fire in her room had been stoked to a blaze of toasty warmth. And Lord Grafton had called her "my love."

She leaned back with a sigh. Perhaps it was merely the strain of the situation that caused him to speak with such sweetness. He might only be relieved that she was safe. She might very well have been killed.

A chill raced down her spine when she remembered the cold hatred in Lady Willow's insane stare. The woman had said that Alaric had loved her. Lucinda's heart was heavy with sadness. All he had done for her, providing for her family and her future, had been done out of love. She felt humbled, but she could not have returned his feelings. Alaric had never been the right man for her.

Her mother felt her forehead. "No fever, but you are still cold to the touch. Snuggle down under the covers, dearest."

"Yes, Mama." She did as bid and her eyes felt heavy.

"Do not sleep yet, dear, not until after the doctor comes. Now tell me from the very beginning what this is all about."

Her mother looked terribly concerned but not crushed with worry. Lucinda began the sordid tale where it started, with the flasks of poisoned brandy that she received as a wedding gift.

Grafton sat behind his desk in the study, completely drained. It had been a long day but a satisfying one, considering they had finally caught Lady Willow and she had confessed in front of the constable. Sir Alaric could finally rest in peace, for his murderer had been found and justice would be served.

Shocked by the scandal, the Wakehams and Lindleys packed their bags into the Darrow sleigh and left for Ivy Park before darkness fell. Mr. Lewes planned to leave as soon as the roads were clear. He informed whoever would listen that his solicitor would hear about this.

And poor Sir Leonard. He looked understandably bewildered when he followed the constable who escorted his wife to jail. He had been abominably used just as Sylvia Harris and her brother, John, had been for Lady Willow's evil revenge. All were headed to court and Lady Willow might end her days in an asylum if she did not hang.

Either way, it was over for him and for Lucinda. He took a deep pull from his small goblet of brandy. Lucinda would no doubt wish to leave this nightmare behind and return home to Bronley Manor, unless—

A knock at the door scattered his thoughts. "Come in."

"Might we speak?" Lucinda stood in the doorway. Her hair was pulled back and she wore a simple dress with a warm shawl wrapped around her shoulders.

He stood, suddenly nervous. "It is late."

She looked hurt and backed away, ready to leave.

He could have kicked himself. "Don't go." He gestured for her to enter. "I simply meant—that is to say, I am surprised you are awake." He felt terribly awkward with her—like a green schoolboy with his first *tendre*.

"I could no longer sleep and I wished to know all that had happened. My mother said that Lady Willow had been caught and that Lady Darrow was involved somehow, but that is all I know." She sat down in the chair nearest the fire.

He came around from behind his desk and sat in the chair next to her. He needed to touch her, so he took her hands into his. "How are you feeling? The doctor said it might take a couple of days before you are rid of the poison and the headaches."

"I feel a little weak, but otherwise no worse for the wear." Her eyes narrowed. "I know Lady Willow was trying to exact revenge on Alaric, but how did she do it all, the cut saddle girth, the gunshot in the woods?"

He leaned back. "Would you like some brandy?"

She wrinkled her nose. "No, thank you. I do not think I will ever go near the stuff."

He smiled. "Of course not. Forgive me. Some wine perhaps? I can ring for tea." Too late he remembered that was how Lady Willow had slowly poisoned her, to make her appear ill.

"The household has been in an uproar. Let your servants rest. I am fine."

And thoughtful, caring, beautiful. He could think of a thousand words to describe her. How infinitely dear she had become when he feared he might have lost her. His heart twisted inside his chest. He did not wish to lose her . . . ever.

"Grafton?" She stroked his cheek. "You look worn to a shade. Perhaps we should table the conversation until morning."

He shook his head. "I doubt I'll sleep well tonight."

Her eyes widened with surprise and understanding. "Sometimes a firm hand helps when you discuss something painful." She repeated the words he once told her with a comforting squeeze of her hand.

He threaded his fingers through hers. "John Harris, the coachman you saw with Lady Darrow, is her brother. Their parents, genteel shopkeepers, died in a fire. They lost everything and John and Sylvia needed work. They were both employed by Sir Reginald Teasedale but he soon made repeated advances toward Sylvia.

"John's skill with the ribbons was well known. In fact, Lord Willow lost to John in a carriage race and offered the coachman considerably higher wages to leave Sir Reginald's. John jumped at the chance and begged Lady Willow to hire his sister. Lady Willow did so, but there was a price to pay. Lady Willow poisoned her husband and forced John into faking a carriage crash so Willow's death would appear to be an accident. If John said a word about it, Lady Willow threatened to cast out Sylvia with poor references. If he did as she asked, then she promised to give his sister a sizable dowry and sponsor a come-out in Bath.

"John had vowed to protect his sister and so he did the only thing he thought he could."

"Poor Mr. Harris," Lucinda whispered.

"Indeed. In Bath, Lady Willow introduced Sylvia to Alaric's nephew and they married. After Sylvia became Mrs. Darrow, John, desperate to leave Lady Willow's employ, went with his sister, keeping their family ties secret. But Lady Willow had another job for John Harris."

"Driving the carriage on my wedding day?"

"Exactly so. Once again, Lady Willow laced flasks of brandy with arsenic with the intent to kill you both and make it look like another carriage accident."

"But I did not drink it."

"Indeed. Lady Willow blackmailed John into cutting your saddle girth, threatening to uncover Sylvia~

as a fraud. But he refused to take a shot at you in the woods. He knew we were looking into your fall from Ariel and it would appear too suspicious. Mr. Dawson had been to Ivy Park to see what he could find.

"John must have told Lady Willow but she was bent on harming you. The shot in the woods, the toy, and then the slow poisoning."

"She shot me?"

"She had come to Ivy Park the day before Christmas Eve."

Lucinda remained quiet.

"That night you saw Lady Darrow with her brother?"

"Yes."

"They were trying to find a way to escape from Lady Willow's clutches. They had hoped to take enough of Alaric's money to run away to the Americas."

"No wonder Lady Darrow was disappointed when most of it was left to me," Lucinda said softly.

"Exactly so, making things more difficult. Lady Darrow had to play a waiting game until she could scrape together the funds. She knew you were in danger but feared for her brother's life if she spoke out."

Lucinda looked into his eyes. "What will happen to them?"

"That is for the magistrate to decide. It will go hard for Lady Willow—that much is certain."

Lucinda shook her head. "How terribly sad."

He cocked his eyebrow in surprise. "Sad?"

Lucinda looked into his eyes. "She was completely

insane. Had you not come upon our carriage accident, I shudder to think what might have happened."

"Right place at the right time," he said. He did not care to think about the alternatives.

"You have gone far above your gentlemanly duty and I thank you."

"A promise given to Sir Alaric to protect you and I swore an oath to find his killer."

"Both you have done admirably." She nodded.

"I would not exactly say that, Lucinda. I failed you."

"You did not."

He looked away. "I was not there to protect you from Lady Willow. You had to deal with her attack alone."

Lucinda's cheeks grew rosy. "But I thought of you and that gave me the strength to get away from her."

Warmth washed over him. Her admission bolstered his courage. Perhaps she truly cared for him. He slipped out of his chair and knelt at her feet. "Lucinda," he whispered, "I . . ."

He was a coward.

"Yes?" She sat on the very edge of her seat.

"I want to kiss you." He did not wait for permission. He pulled her close and his mouth sought hers. He intended to be gentle but once her fingers sank into his hair, he lost all reason. His lips demanded response and he groaned when she answered in kind.

Lucinda opened to his insistent tongue that teased her bottom lip until she could stand it no more. She drank in the worship he paid to her mouth and did not care how inappropriate her actions. This time, she held nothing back when she kissed him. All her fears and feelings and frustrations melded into a desperate plea. She loved him and she wanted him to love her in return.

"Sweet, incredibly beautiful Lucinda," he murmured against her neck, setting fire with a trail of hot kisses along her jaw.

"Grafton?" She needed to know where she stood before she could continue. Just what were his intentions?

"Hmmmmmm?" He nibbled her earlobe.

"Please, stop, dearest." She gripped his shoulders, then ran her fingers down the back of his shirt.

It was not the best move. He pulled her closer and she slipped out of the chair to kneel upon the carpeted floor with him.

"Grafton." She was nearly incoherent with wanting him. "Why—why do you kiss me so?"

That stopped him cold. He pulled back and searched her face. "Do you not want me to?"

Lucinda looked at him and sighed. His hair was tousled and mussed and his eyes were wide and innocent. She bit her lip. "That is not the point." She took a deep breath. "The point is that I do not know what your feelings are toward me and—"

He captured her face with both his hands. "I love you."

She was elated, stunned. "You do?"

He smiled. "I do."

She was speechless. His sentiments so simply said took her breath away, even her heart skipped a beat.

"Now, then, are you ready to really kiss me?" he said with a mischievous wink.

She took another deep breath. He was always so

proper and this was definitely improper and completely tempting. "I do not know."

"I want to marry you."

Relieved, she flung her arms around his neck. "Oh, Grafton." She planted her lips firmly on his and kissed him without shame. Then she *really* kissed him.

When they finally broke apart for air, he asked, "Should I assume that means yes?"

She giggled. "Yes, my love, yes. I will marry you but I think I should like to kiss you once again."

So he obliged her.

And then she pulled back again. "Dearest, we had best stop or it will be a very long eleven months ahead."

"What?" His gray eyes were dark and dreamy with desire.

"Before we can marry."

He shook his head. "No."

"What do you mean 'no'?"

"We will not wait eleven months to wed." He gave her a saucy smile.

"But what will people think?"

"I don't give a hang what they think." He looked sheepish, then explained, "Lucinda, life is too precious to waste time worrying about convention. We need each other now. I will send Robbie for a special license and we can be married by Twelfth Night."

Her eyes widened with surprise and then she smiled. She agreed with him wholeheartedly. It would be another infamous wedding for Lucinda Bronwell, only this time she had the right man.

Two anthologies of Christmas novellas
to warm your heart—from
your favorite Regency authors.

Regency Christmas Courtship
stories by
**Barbara Metzger, Edith Layton,
Andrea Pickens, Nancy Butler,
and Gayle Buck**
0-451-21681-4

Regency Christmas Wishes
stories by
**Sandra Heath, Emma Jensen,
Carla Kelly, Edith Layton,
and Barbara Metzger**
0-451-21044-1

Available wherever books are sold or at
penguin.com

Also by
Jenna Mindel

Miss Whitlow's Turn

0-451-21035-2

Miss Harriet Whitlow's father wishes to see her
married to a wealthy nobleman—but her heart belongs
to George Clasby, a rake who wishes to reform.
Now she must throw caution to the wind and find
the courage to fulfill her heart's desire.

Kiss of the Highwayman

0-451-21034-4

When Artemis Rothwell travels to London for her
coming out, notorious highwaymen rob her of a
precious ring. But one thief kisses Artemis—whispering
that he'll restore it. Now she longs for the masked
man to fulfill his promise.

**Available wherever books are sold or at
penguin.com**

s552

Now available from
REGENCY ROMANCE

When Horses Fly
by Laurie Bishop
Cantankerous Lord Wintercroft has taken in Cora, a
poor relation and nurse, to live in his decrepit stone
castle and, eventually, to wed. But the nurse, herself, is
lovesick for Wintercroft's son, Alex.

0-451-21682-2

A Singular Lady
by Megan Frampton
Recently impoverished orphan Titania Stanhope must
marry money if she plans to survive. The Earl of
Oakley has money, but, in an attempt to keep gold-dig-
ging girls at bay, keeps it a secret. Then he meets
Titania, whose sharp wit and keen mind are rivaled
only by her lovely face.

0-451-21683-0

My Lady Gamester
by Cara King
A bankrupt lady with a thirst for risk sets her sites on
a new mark—the Earl of Stoke. Now she has to take
him for all he's worth—without losing her heart.

0-451-21719-5